THE LAST DANCE

THE LAST DANCE

Justice in Small-Town America

Book Two of the Dancing Deer Series

By Ron Lambert

Published in the United States by:

Printers Guild Publishing House

425 Spring Street, Suite 101
Columbus, Texas 78934-2461
Phone (979)732-2962   Fax (979)733-0015
www.printersguildpublshing.com

ISBN 978-0-9855083-2-6

The Last Dance is a work of Fiction

Dancing Deer is not an actual town. It is a composite of several towns the author has visited. In his stories he occasionally used the actual names of other Arkansas' towns and scenic wonders in passing.

Except for some historical personages the names, characters, and incidents of his stories are used fictitiously and do not represent any actual person or event.

Since some of the towns, cities, or geographic localities are real, an interested reader might be able to locate Lee Mountain, Moccasin Gap, the Buffalo River, the Big Piney, and numerous other places or items mentioned. Eudy's Drug and Fountain might be harder.

The author grew up in a small rural community and saw wonder in all living things.

Trademarks

Cover

Picture by Shutterstock.com

Contents

CHAPTER 1—THE CRIME

February 17, 1945

At four a.m. on a cold and windy Saturday in northern Arkansas a sleepy police dispatcher was startled awake by a calm voice whispering a man lay dead on one of Dancing Deer's residential streets. A squad car was dispatched with its siren wailing. Another call was made, this one from the police dispatcher to the Dancing Deer Chief of Police, W. W. Wainwright, and another to the Marsden County Coroner.

Wayne Winchell Wainwright had moved to Dancing Deer through an ad he found in the *Law Enforcement Journal*. He was tired of big city crime. He wanted to spend the last few years of his career in a place without much crime and without much work. Wainwright thought Dancing Deer was it. He'd been in this sleepy little town four years and, if this was a homicide, it would be his first on the new job. He dragged himself out of bed. When he got to the scene he was on a street containing six small apartment buildings, three on each side. A patrol unit had set up spotlights, roped off the area, stretched tarps to shield the body from onlookers, and was diligently keeping the curious away from the crime scene. Across the street Sheriff Sherman Shodtoe watched from the window of his third-floor apartment.

To the officer in charge the chief asked, "Has the body been touched?"

"No, sir. The coroner hasn't arrived. The only thing we've done is set a patrolman at the front and rear of this center building and another inside to talk to its occupants. We've got two men talking with the occupants of the other five buildings. In the meantime I'm canvassing the grassy area looking for anything that might prove useful."

Chief Wainwright inspected the body. It was sprawled out like it was trying to crawl up a fence lying flat on the ground. There was a hole in the back of the victim's head where the slug exited. A hat that snapped to the bill clung to matted hair with dried blood camouflaging the transition from flesh to hair to hat.

"Have you found the slug?"

"Not yet, Chief."

"Have you found any bone fragments?"

"Yes, sir. On the sidewalk."

"Anything else?"

"A footprint in the blood beside the body. It's a man's right dress shoe."

"Have somebody go through the people outside the rope. Get names. Look at their shoes."

The chief knew most perps liked to return to the scene of the crime. There must be some magnet that drew them. Maybe they got off on being close to their handiwork or close to the people looking for them, like a catch-me-if-you-can adrenalin rush.

Another car arrived and the county coroner lumbered over to look at the body. "My God. It's a homicide."

"What did you expect?" asked Chief Wainwright.

"I dunno. I operate the funeral home. This is my first homicide."

"Aren't you the county coroner?"

"Yeah. Name's Thaddeus Wilke." He held out his hand. "Just elected. You don't become county coroner through experience, rather through political associations."

The chief held out his hand. "Chief Wainwright."

Wilke went back to his car and retrieved a briefcase and a leather box with a handle. In a few minutes he'd taken several pictures of the body, wrapped a rope around its outline, and took the temperature of its liver with an invasive thermometer. He used a different thermometer to take the outside temperature. In an hour he'd prepared his preliminary report and had the body loaded in an ambulance headed for an autopsy at his funeral home. Only a bright yellow tape replacing the rope remained and yellow markers for evidence found by the police.

In his leather box he put back the remaining roll of tape, the bright yellow rope, a tape measure, a pair of calipers, two thermometers, and two rolls of film. In his briefcase he put his list detailing the pictures taken in their proper sequence and other notes he'd made. This might be his first homicide, but he knew the procedure.

A patrolman charged out of the apartment building. He went straight to his boss. "We got another one, Chief. A woman."

"Go tell the coroner. I think he's about to leave with the first body."

Chief Wainwright entered the apartment building. He'd been there before. A feeling of horror engulfed his body. He bounded up the steps to the second floor and saw the door open. He grabbed a handrail while standing on the last step. A light from the room cast an oblong rectangle on the carpeted floor. Steadying himself Chief Wainwright bit down on his bottom lip and walked to the open door.

Deputy Chief Steve Trent, wearing thin rubber gloves and carrying a notepad, was gathering fingerprints from likely places. An auburn-haired woman in her early thirties lay dead on the bed in a black negligee.

Trent stopped work and said, "I told the other occupants to stay in their rooms and not to make any telephone calls. I have their names. No one has owned up to hearing a thing. The woman's name is Raylene Carlisle."

"I know who she is."

Prostitution is the art of selling sex. When Raylene got off the bus in Dancing Deer ten years earlier, she decided prostitution was the means by which she would make her mark on the world. Her mother was sick and had pawned the only thing she had of value, her wedding ring, for Raylene's bus fare out. Raylene's father had deserted them years before, leaving her mother with a cynical attitude and very little else. She gave Raylene the three axioms by which Raylene would live her life: men are shallow, love is make-believe, and nothing is permanent.

Raylene got a job at the local diner while she figured out how she would attract her paying customers. Her salary would allow her to live in a boarding house with very little left and that was another problem Raylene had to solve. There was only one motel. It was on the highway at the outskirts of town. If she took her customers there, it would just be a short while before she became known. Raylene didn't want that; she wanted to ply her trade with only the few well-heeled paying customers knowing. So Raylene worked at her job and rebuffed all attempts by the boys wanting for free what she was making plans to sell.

Raylene opened a bank account and met the bank president, Bill Potter. He was the type of customer she wanted. From the small amount of social talk she had managed to squeeze out, Raylene learned Potter was into politics, raising a little girl, and liked his steak medium-rare. Raylene joined the *Young Republicans* organization and helped with fundraisers. At election time she canvassed the neighborhoods giving out leaflets for Republican nominees. On occasion she worked alongside Mr. Potter.

"What have you done with Mrs. Potter? I haven't seen her at any of our functions."

"Miss Carlisle, my wife lives in Boston. After being immersed in the trappings of the big city, she couldn't take our small-town lifestyle. She left ten years ago."

"I'm sorry. I didn't mean to pry. Maybe you need a new love interest. Someone who likes living in a small town."

Bill picked up a stack of index cards listing people who had donated to the Republican cause.

Raylene continued, "Mr. Potter . . . uh, Bill. What do you like to do socially?"

"Raylene, I'm old enough to be your father. How old are you? Twenty? If I were to see you socially, people would talk . . ."

"I'm twenty-four and people wouldn't have to know."

Bill put down the cards. He looked at the attractive woman with long, curly hair and reclassified her—from friend to possible playmate.

"Look, have your daughter sleep over with one of her girlfriends and I'll come by and cook your dinner. We can discuss it."

What was eventually decided was that they would have a sexual relationship on Friday evenings. No strings attached. In return for Raylene being available every Friday night, Bill would pay her one hundred dollars, rent her an apartment, and help get it furnished. No one was to know of their arrangement and either could terminate it at any time.

After two months Raylene decided her relationship with Bill was working out so well she needed to expand, find someone else for another night or two during the week. Raylene switched parties. Dancing Deer was Democratic. Most of the elected officials were Democrats. So when Raylene joined the *Coalition for a More Democratic Government* she started meeting a larger number of potential customers. She wasn't interested in dating someone her own age. She wasn't interested in getting married. What Raylene was interested in was gaining a Monday and a Wednesday.

The ones she chose were a lonely, retired baseball player and an up-and-coming lawyer. The first a widower and the second a confirmed bachelor and both agreeable to a little something on the side. Raylene was careful to keep each unaware of any other. With the amount charged, Raylene could finally afford to quit her job at the diner. That's when she met Daniel.

Daniel Poul was two years younger than Raylene. He fell head over heels in love with her at first sight. She let him take her to the fair when it came to town in September. They rode the make-shift rides, ate cotton candy, and threw rings at bottles. Daniel won Raylene a kewpie doll by knocking three heavy milk bottles off a small table from about twelve feet. Raylene now had paying customers for Monday, Wednesday, and Friday evenings and one she worked for free on weekends. She was buying condoms in the large economy-sized box.

Daniel lived with his parents and when the old woman next door died he ransacked her house. He'd heard the woman rant about the banker and reasoned she had her savings hidden somewhere in the house. At first he carefully looked through her things, putting back everything as he found it. As time went on and nothing appeared Daniel started getting careless and then reckless. Before long he was upset and began tossing hatboxes, dresser drawers, books, and pieces of furniture. Then he found it. Ten thousand dollars in fifty and hundred-dollar bills. Daniel stuffed the money and a man's watch in his pockets and ran from the house.

When he came to his senses Daniel decided if he was caught he'd go to jail. Her relatives probably knew the old woman had money hidden and would be upset when they arrived looking for her will and found someone had rifled through her things. He went to Raylene's.

Daniel was not to come unless it was a weekend but to hell with her rules. He had to have Raylene hide his money.

"Daniel. What are you doing here? I've told you under no circumstances were you to come to my apartment. Were you not paying attention?"

"Raylene, honey, I've just got a minute and then I'll be on my way. Can we talk?"

"If you make it snappy."

"I need for you to keep something for me. Do you have a sack or a box?"

Raylene left, bringing back a shoebox. Daniel pulled money out of four pockets and dumped it inside the box.

"Where'd you get all this money?"

"It's mine. I just need a place to hide it for a spell." Daniel kissed Raylene and shot out the door.

A man walking his dog had seen Daniel running from the old woman's house. When the police started questioning her neighbors the man told them about Daniel. At the trial it was decided that Daniel stole an undetermined and unrecovered amount of money and the watch of the woman's long deceased husband. With two previous misdemeanors and one armed robbery, Daniel was given a fifteen-year sentence.

Four years into his arrangement with Raylene, the single attorney developed a plan to run for governor and broke off their long-term relationship. It was an amicable breakup but it left Raylene with reduced income. After keeping Daniel's money hidden for two years, she started dipping into the shoebox. When the new chief of police from Chicago was hired four years previous she got herself on the welcoming committee and before long the chief was her Wednesday. She then replenished the spent money and opened a savings account with it at the bank.

Chief Wainwright surveyed Raylene's apartment. It had been turned upside down. The killer was looking for something. "Did you find an address book or list of telephone numbers?" Deputy Chief Trent bit his lower lip and shook his head. "Was there a pad of paper with a list of names by the telephone? On her nightstand? Maybe on, or in, her desk?"

"No."

"Did you find a purse?"

"Yeah. It's been dusted and each item listed and boxed for delivery to headquarters."

"You work pretty fast. I hope you're just as thorough." Chief Wainwright walked over and held out his hand for the notebook. "Let me see the list of items."

Officer Trent handed his boss the notebook and continued dusting. When handed back the notebook, Trent made a careful entry where each new print found had been located and its angle of orientation. His operation was to use black magnetic powder on any non-metallic surface. He held anything metal over a canister of burning pine kindling sending up black sooty smoke. When the item had sufficiently cooled he brushed away the excess black soot with a squirrel-bristled brush. Any fingerprints found were covered with a piece of tape and transferred to a card. On the card he entered the location and other bits of necessary information. For paper surfaces he had iodine crystals but so far had not used them.

There was a knock on the open door. A patrolman stood at the entranceway. He knew better than to come in and overpopulate the crime scene. "Sir, we've interviewed everyone in the five other apartment buildings. No one heard any gun shots but there was some activity. A man came out of this building a few minutes before ten walking rather briskly and got into a black Packard touring sedan."

"Was he recognized?"

"No. The witness said he was in a long overcoat and wearing a hat. He didn't see his face."

"You need to get as much information as you can. Memories don't last long. He'll forget half of what he knows by mid-morning."

"Yes, sir. Chief, Sheriff Shodtoe lives in the building across the street. He asked if you would like his assistance."

"You tell that jackass, unless he has some county warrant to deliver, to leave the police work to the professionals."

"Yes, sir."

Thaddeus Wilke walked in with his briefcase and leather box. "Chief, what's going on? We got a crazy man loose or has another war broke out?"

15

"You tell me. When do you think you'll know something?"

"You can have my preliminary report this afternoon. I'll start the autopsies in a couple of hours. Which one do you want first?"

"Raylene, I guess. I want to know specifically if she was raped. And, of course, anything else you can come up with."

Chief Wainwright stood stone still in meditation. It was two minutes before he walked to Raylene's desk. It was the nicest piece of furniture in the apartment: ornate with fancy drawer pulls and leather inlays. The chief thought it was French. "Steve, are you finished over here?"

"I've only done the surfaces of the desk and chair. I didn't find any usable prints. Nothing inside's been touched."

"Okay, I'll wear gloves and put everything back like I found it." Chief Wainwright slowly slid the center drawer open to a stop. It contained an envelope with pictures stuffed in halfway, a checkbook and register, and a stack of letters. He looked through the pictures. There was an old ramshackle house. A little girl playing with a dog. A stooped woman cooking something on a stove. A couple wearing worn and patched clothing. Some shots of scenery. Nothing recent. The pictures were yellowing, already curling on the corners. He put them back inside the envelope and picked up the stack of letters. The return address said they were from a Beatrice Carlisle in an old-folks home in Harrison. He started reading the one with the latest postmark. She visited her mother on weekends once or twice a month. Nothing happening there. He next turned to the checkbook, noting the number of the first remaining check. In the register it appeared all the checks were accounted for. The amounts entered were for normal things: groceries, drug items, beauty salon, Creighton's Jewelers, two hundred dollars per month to the Sunnyside Convalescent Center of Harrison, and bus tickets. Her deposits were regular: three hundred dollars per week. He knew one hundred was from him. Who supplied the remaining amount? He'd have to find out. This wasn't going to be pleasant.

He had once told Raylene he loved her. He'd asked her to marry him. In the next drawer he found a cigar box with a few coins and trinkets. On the right was one large drawer normally used for filing. It contained a dozen love-story books. He thought it must be where she

16

got her ideas. Every Wednesday night she would have a delightful meal prepared. Raylene liked to have the lamps turned down or off with candles providing what light they needed. Sometimes they played games or listened to the radio or phonograph. Other times she had scribbled acting scenes on tablets of paper. She always had her lines memorized. Raylene must've spent hours coming up with bedroom trysts and lover's spats that would have to be reconciled in the bedroom. He loved the efforts she made to entertain him.

Sometimes she would sit on his lap, cradle his face with her hands, and sing him love songs she had written. Whoever killed Raylene would pay. He would pay with his life. If he didn't fry in "Old Spanky," W.W. vowed he'd kill him with his fists and say the man had been resisting arrest.

Chief Wainwright observed the coroner inspecting Raylene's body and decided he needed to leave. "Steve, I'm going to interview the other residents. Give Mr. Wilke a hand if he needs anything." The chief gave a quick look around the bedroom. "Where's the second pillow?"

"Damned if I know. I didn't realize we were one short. I'll mention it in my notes."

The chief headed for the front door. Officer Trent yelled out, "Chief, I think that man outside is Katy Hamelin's husband. I've only seen hats like he's wearing on people from up north and I haven't heard of any other non-natives in town."

The chief said, "I think you're right. We'll have Mrs. Hamelin view the body after Mr. Wilke is finished with the autopsy."

After interviewing the tenants on the first and second floor, Chief Wainwright wearily walked up the last flight of stairs with no new information. The second apartment he knocked on belonged to Faye Spencer.

"Miss Spencer, did you hear anyone arguing or a gun shot last night or early this morning?" Chief Wainwright walked into her living room. He casually looked around.

"No, Chief. These walls are pretty thick. We didn't hear anything." Faye walked over and sat on the sofa. "Please, Chief. Have a seat. You look weary."

"Thank you. I am."

Katy came in from the bedroom. "Do you know who the victim was?"

"Not yet. He didn't have any identification in his pockets. However, he might be your husband. I'll need for you to come down to the Rest In Peace Funeral Home and see if you can identify the body. Will that be all right?"

"Yes. I'll do whatever you want." She dabbed at her eyes with a handkerchief. "I don't know if I want it to be Galen or not. We were married for many unhappy years. But he was still my husband and we were happy the first few." She paused a moment. "How was he killed?" Katy sat on the sofa beside her sister.

"Shot in the head from close range." The chief took out a small rectangular card from his vest pocket. "Here's my card. Call me if you think of anything that might be important. I'll have a squad car pick you up when the coroner gives permission. In the meantime, each of you write down on a separate sheet of paper everything you did yesterday through this morning. Officer Trent will come by later and pick them up. He might have more questions."

Faye said, "Chief Wainwright, may I interview you for the paper? How about pictures?"

"I think someone from the paper has already been taking pictures. We've had to ask him and Mr. Bell to step behind the boundary tape twice. Come by my office this afternoon and I'll give you a statement you can print."

The chief thanked the ladies and left for the diner. He needed a cup of coffee. If the man was Katy's husband that might account for why he was there. But why kill Raylene? Both Faye and Katy were visibly upset. Maybe, there's more to their story than simply an abusive husband trying to retrieve a runaway wife.

On the way out the chief poked his head in Raylene's apartment. "Steve, you know anyone who drives a Packard sedan?"

"Bill Potter."

CHAPTER 2—BILL POTTER

February 8, 1945 (nine days before the double murder)

The house hated him. It was time to leave. Three years earlier Bill had started construction on the Ritz Grand Hotel and Ballroom. He'd always planned on moving into its penthouse but when his daughter, Rose, ran away he couldn't make any changes. He wanted to be around his things—her things. He wanted everything to be the way it had been, so he procrastinated. Now that she was back, married to that Calhoun kid and living in Fayetteville, it was time for him to move to the hotel.

"I'll tell you what I'm going to do. I'm going to sell you to someone I don't like." Bill grinned and thought about qualifying people. "I'll figure out who I hate the most, someone from out of town—one of those Bond's boys from Wind Springs maybe—and offer him a deal so good he'll snap you up in a minute and let you sit vacant."

Bill walked outside and stuck a sign in the front yard. He would have the last word. Lately, he'd found lights on in rooms he seldom used; things not in their normal places; shadows moving in dark corners; and flecks of light barely perceptible from the corner of his eye.

"Look, I couldn't help it. She's gone to live with her husband. You'll have to get over it."

Bill reached for his hat. From its resting place on the hat rack it fell to the floor. Bill rolled his eyes and walked out, pulling the door behind him. The door slammed shut. Bill stopped and turned around facing the house. "I might have a bulldozer level you to the ground."

Besides owning the hotel, and a few other businesses, Bill was president of the First Bank and Trust of Dancing Deer. Seated in a sumptuous leather chair, he considered what the day had in store. He told his secretary he wanted to talk to Charles Jimmerson, his new recruit in charge of real estate, pronto. He mulled over the latest turn of events. Old man Ridley was holding out on his parcel of land with the thermal spring. Somehow he'd figured out what a valuable asset he owned and rebuffed the purchase offers tendered.

Carla brought in a tray holding a coffee carafe, two cups, and two newspapers. Bill subscribed to the *Kansas City Star* and the *St. Louis Dispatch*. They arrived every day with the mail and were only two days old. This is how he started his day: employees hopping, a cup of hot coffee, and a wealth of information.

"Mr. Jimmerson said he had a meeting with Mr. Ridley this morning. I don't expect him back before ten," said Carla.

"I hope we can start to see some headway soon. How about the plans for the public restrooms?" Bill sipped his coffee. It was still too hot to drink.

"The architects said they need the site dimensions. You'll have to find that out at the next city council meeting."

"Thanks."

Bill reached for his coffee, decided to wait another minute, and picked up one of the papers. Two months earlier he'd owned up to a particularly brutal act of revenge he once perpetrated on his daughter's new father-in-law. To atone for his misdeeds he'd promised Jed Calhoun, David's father, he'd do several anonymous projects for the city. He'd already fixed the clock on the county courthouse, planted trees, and repaired the sidewalks. The town was now balking at the remaining items on his list. They wanted to know who was buying out their town. They couldn't believe anyone would pony up money for them and not expect something in return.

Later that morning Bill walked to his hotel and took the elevator to the top floor. The door wouldn't open until he inserted his key. When Bill walked out he was in his new living room. He'd hired an interior decorator to completely furnish it according to his new tastes. It now contained paintings of western scenes, two Remington sculptures, and was full of leather furniture. He even had leather inlays in the tables. The last few months he'd started sporting western clothing. It was ready for him to move in. He just needed to bring over his clothes and a shaving kit.

Bill looked around in approval. It was a big suite of rooms with a kitchen—the only kitchen in the entire hotel if you didn't count the one for the bistro on the ground floor. Besides a large living room there were two bedrooms and a bath for each, with one of the baths also opening onto the hall. It had an office and a dining room with windows and a door opening onto a balcony overlooking Main Street from four floors up.

Downstairs, he went to his regular table in the Ritz Hotel Bistro and ordered lunch. Charles Jimmerson walked up and stood beside a vacant chair.

"Sir, I have an counter offer from Mr. Ridley. It's a little high. I think if we wait he'll come down to our last bid."

"That's great, Jimmerson. Have a seat. Have you had lunch?"

"No, sir. I came looking for you as soon as he gave me his figure. It's really not out of the ballpark considering it's on Main Street—and with a thermal spring."

"Does he know who he's selling it to?"

"No. I told him it was someone from out of town. They'd just asked for the bank's assistance. And after landscaping the property into a park, it would be donated back to the city."

"Take the offer. Draw up the papers using that dummy corporation. Tell Carla how much money you'll need. She'll take it from there. Make out the contract this afternoon and send it to Jellico to look over. You'll need to deliver it to Ridley as soon as you get it back. In the meantime have the Dancing Deer Title Company run a title check. Oh, and have a surveyor stake out the legal boundaries.

"Yes, sir. You sure move fast."

Both men felt good about the transaction and ate in comparative silence, talking only about the weather and whether spring was going to come early. When the meal was over and both men were about to leave, Bill asked, "Charles, have you located a place to live?"

"No, sir. I'm still staying at the boarding house. My wife's living with her parents in Eureka Springs until I find something. We've decided to save up a few paychecks and put a down payment on a small house on the outskirts of town."

"I have a house you might find interesting. It's mine. I'm moving to the hotel and have decided to sell. Why don't you and your wife come look at it this weekend?"

"Mr. Potter, that sounds swell but I don't think we can afford it. We haven't been able to save any money. It took everything we could make to put me through college."

Bill wiped at a water ring on the table with his napkin. Standing up he said, "I might make some concessions for a man who has as bright a future as you. Do you think two o'clock Sunday afternoon would be convenient?"

"Yes, sir. I'll have to bring my little boy."

"You have children?"

"Eston's five. But Mary's pregnant again. This time she thinks it's going to be twins."

"Son, I don't pay you enough money to have a family that big."

"Mr. Potter, you'd be amazed at how far Mary can make a dollar stretch. During my college she cleaned other peoples' houses and took in ironing. Right now she's selling Fuller Brushes. Do you still want us to come look at your house?"

"By all means. I've got to meet this Mary."

Saturday evening Bill looked around his house. What did he need to take, what could he leave behind, and what could he throw away? A knock on the door. Good grief, who would be coming to see him this late at night? When Bill opened the door he couldn't believe his eyes.

"Harriet, what are you doing here?"

"Willie, aren't you going to invite me in? It's been a long trip." She shifted a small makeup bag to her other hand. "You know you'll drown if it rains and you've got your mouth hanging open like that."

Harriet was his ex-wife. They came from Boston to live in Dancing Deer when his father died but she had never considered living in a country town. No theater, no fancy restaurants, no professional baseball. She didn't last long. A month after sweeping in, she swept out, leaving behind their three year-old daughter for him to raise.

"Come in. Let me have your suitcase." Bill took hold of the make-up bag. "Why are you here?"

"I've come to see our grandson. And to check up on you. You never write anymore. Willie, don't you still love me?"

"Harriet, you're the one who left. Abandoned me. I came home from work and the next door neighbor's coloring with our daughter. You left me a three-word note for God's sakes."

"Yes, well, I'm sorry about that. We were both so young. That's all behind us now. Do be a dear and bring in the rest of my luggage. The taxi driver left it sitting on the curb."

"Harriet, you can't move in here. What will people say?"

"Since when have you cared what people say?"

"I've changed." Bill looked over her shoulder to the street. There were six large suitcases beside his mailbox. "Harriet, we need to get you to the hotel."

"Oh, posh. I'll go later. Rose told me you've mellowed out. You're a lot nicer than you used to be. I had to come see for myself. Could we drive to Fayetteville tomorrow? I've got to see little Carson. One of those suitcases is for him. It's full of toys and little boy's clothes."

Bill took her things to the guest's bedroom. This wasn't going to work. Faye Spencer was just beginning to see things his way and, he knew for sure, she wasn't going to like his ex-wife complicating things.

"I've got someone coming to look at the house tomorrow afternoon. We can go to Fayetteville as soon as they leave."

Harriet went into the kitchen, grabbed an apron, and looked in the refrigerator to see if there might be anything worth fixing. When Bill went to bed he locked his bedroom door. He had to regain control of the situation.

By one o'clock Sunday afternoon Harriet had already cooked Bill two meals and tidied up his house. She spent thirty minutes cleaning his bathroom. He ended up showering in the hall bathroom and sneaking into his bedroom wrapped in a towel.

"My, but aren't we modest."

Harriet sat down in a bedroom chair to watch him get dressed. Bill got a pair of socks and underwear from a chest of drawers and stepped into his walk-in closet. He had to get dressed in the dark when Harriet turned off the closet light. When he emerged he was wearing a navy blue shirt and black slacks. He turned on the light a second time and went back for a red and black striped sport shirt, jeans, and black boots.

23

Charles and his family arrived while Bill was napping in a big leather chair. He awoke when Harriet started showing them around. Bill went into the living room and Harriet excused herself, making a hasty retreat to the guest bedroom.

Charles said, "Mr. Potter, this is my wife, Mary, and our son, Eston."

"I'm glad to meet you both." Bill yawned, covered his mouth, and shook his head. After regaining his composure he said, "I'm sorry. I've been asleep." He paused. "Mary, what do you think of our neighborhood? There's lots of little boys. I sometimes see them playing marbles."

Mary was holding Charles' hand. "Mr. Potter, the neighborhood's wonderful. This is a very nice house. One we might like to own someday, but it's beyond our budget right now. And we don't have but a few pieces of furniture."

"I completely understand."

The foyer light came on. The Jimmersons looked toward the front door expecting to see someone at the light switch.

"I've had that switch checked and the electrician says it's wired properly. I don't know why it comes on by itself. Why don't I show you the house and then we'll see what we can do about its price."

Harriet came out of the bedroom with a toy fire truck. "Do you think your son would like to play with this while Willie and I show you the house?"

Before Eston's parents could say anything he had the fire truck and was rolling it around the living room floor. Bill walked to the door from the dining room opening onto the back yard. He hesitated before trying the knob. Lately the door had been sticking. This time it almost jumped open when he touched the handle.

"I've got a nice large lot with plenty of room for children to play. Lots of shade trees. You might want to build Eston a tree house in that live oak." Bill pointed to a giant tree with massive low-hanging branches.

In a few minutes they had been through every room in the house. Bill marveled to himself at how the windows opened and closed

24

at the slightest touch, how the tile in the kitchen sparkled in the ray of sunlight coming through the window.

"Okay, here's what I propose. You rent the house first. Just give me a week to get moved to the hotel. You can keep any of the furniture you want. Donate anything extra to a local church. I'll consider the monthly rent as a pay raise to Charles. If, in a couple of years, you want to buy the house, we'll have it appraised and that'll be its selling price. At that time Charles and I will renegotiate his salary. In the meantime you can start saving for the down payment. Does that sound like a deal to you?"

Galen Hamelin had been on the road for weeks. He'd walked, hitched, and stowed in train cars. He arrived in Dancing Deer on Monday morning, February 12, 1945.

Galen thought, where's that woman? She should know better than to run off leaving me holding the bag. With her fifty thousand I could pay off my debts and we could start over somewhere else. We could even go back to Chicago. Live with civilized people for a change. This has got to be the place. Faye is the only family left now her dad's dead. The old geezer left her just enough money to get my butt out of hock.

Sure, we've had our problems—not what you'd call a happy family. We're on the run. We've already sneaked out of Chicago to Kansas City. Katy didn't like being yanked around but what was I to do? I couldn't pay and the interest was outta sight. How the hell do they expect me to pay 'em back if they won't front me any more money? I'm a gambler. If I don't have any money I can't make any money. If they find me now they'll kill me for sure. Paying them off before I'm found is the only way.

Dancing Deer is so stinking small I'll locate her easy. Wander around. Keep my eyes peeled. I'll spot her and whisk her, and her stash away before anyone's aware of what's going on. Now that I've got a little money. Damn, they should've had more in the till. A hundred dollars. One stinking hundred dollars. And ten of that in the apron of the waitress.

Once I get Katy's money and pay Big Ed, I'll get a real job. This is no way to live. I'll show her I'm not the loser she says I am. I've just been down on my luck. None of my horses come in; the dice won't fall; my cards have all bust. I've had a long streak of bad luck. Well, with Katy's money, things are going to change.

There any pool halls in this town? Any joints?

Galen Hamelin pulled his coat tight, put his hands in his pockets, and walked down Main Street. When he could he stayed close to the buildings, in the shadows. He kept his head down except when he spied a group of people. A quick look-see and then head down and farther along the sidewalk. He'd been from one end of Main Street to the other without seeing her. He was now walking side streets. The wind whistled.

Cold? They call this cold? When that wind comes blowing in off Lake Michigan, that's cold. This ain't nothing. Galen spied a drunk picking up trash and walked over for a chat. "Hey, buddy. There any action around?"

The drunk pulled a white sock down over his ears. "What are you talking about? Action? I don't know anything about any action." He pulled a mason jar out of his coat pocket, used a fingerless glove to unscrew the lid, and took a swig. He offered the jar to Galen.

"Yeah, don't mind if I do. Say, you know a Faye Spencer? Tall, redhead, in her thirties."

"Naw."

"She might be working for a newspaper."

"Naw. Gimme back the shine."

"Take it easy, old-timer. Here. Any pool halls around?"

"Yeah. That way about a mile. They don't let 'em be in town. Too uppity."

On the way to the pool hall Galen stopped at a run-down café. On the counter beside the till was a stack of newspapers. He placed a dime in a cup and took the top paper to a booth.

"What the hell is chicken-fried steak? Is it chicken, fried like you would a steak or, maybe, a steak, cooked like fried chicken?" Galen folded the menu and crammed it between the sugar and a napkin holder.

The waitress looked down at him. "You got any money?"

"Yeah. You got any food?"

"Let me see your money. We don't want no vagrants stiffing us."

He'd been on the road for a couple of weeks. He hadn't thought to pack any clothes. He later decided it was just as well. This way he didn't have anything getting in his way, nothing to keep up with. Until he robbed that diner he hadn't had any money either. He'd rolled a few drunks but they didn't have any money. He'd slept under bridges and stole food from houses left unattended. But he had money now. He reached into his pocket and pulled out a wad of bills.

The woman left. In a minute she returned with a glass of water. "It's a thin steak battered, deep-fried, and served covered with milk-gravy. Our cook's from Alabama. She says that's all they eat down there—and fried chicken of course."

"Okay, I'll have chicken-fried steak, fried potatoes, and a beer. You got something on draft?"

"No beer. You'll have to get that at Snockered."

"Snockered?"

"Yeah, it's a pool hall up the road a piece. We only sell alcohol in this county if you belong to a club."

"Well, what you got?"

"We got iced tea—sweet and unsweet."

"I'll drink water."

Galen looked at the front page of the newspaper. Right there was an article about someone having the sidewalks rebuilt, written by Faye Spencer. This'll be easy. Tomorrow I'll find the newspaper's office and follow Faye home. That's where Katy will be.

It was Valentine's day and Faye sat in a corner and listened. She had her notebook and several sharp pencils. Bill was the only one paying her any attention. Every time she looked his way he was smiling. They were in the Dancing Deer City Council Chambers with the members discussing the latest act of charity by an anonymous donor.

"I'm here to tell you there are no free rides. No one's going to foot the bill for these public outhouses and not expect something in return." Harold Greenleaf plopped his hefty frame down. He had been on the city council four terms. During that time he had tacitly agreed with whatever the majority wanted, seldom expressing a dissenting opinion. But this latest act of charity rubbed him the wrong way. From his chair Harold added, "I didn't object when those trees got planted, when that clock repair guy fixed the town clock, or when sneaky Pete had the sidewalks rebuilt and expanded, but I've now got to draw the line. So far he, or maybe she, hasn't asked us for a damn thing, but I think we're being lured down a dark alley with the offer of a bit of candy."

Bill got to his feet. "Gentlemen, I can assure you this gentle benefactor only wants to help the city. No one can argue that it's not a more beautiful city with the trees and new sidewalks. I think we ought to let this person spend his, or her, money on us. If he wants to keep his identity secret it probably means he wants to decide what civic projects get funded and not be pressured by local politicians looking to enhance their holdings by subverting the funds to something giving them undue benefit." Bill sat down.

Paul Nelson was the next to offer his opinion. "I like the way the city looks as it is. I don't want some foreigner coming in here changing things. I've heard in Oklahoma City they've started putting parking meters on the curbs, making people pay to park. I don't want Dancing Deer to be like that. I want to keep it small and cozy. If we let this person spruce it up, there'll be a horde of people sneaking in buying all the available buildings and empty lots. Before long we won't recognize our little town. I say we put a stop to accepting any more charity."

The council meeting closed with a vote of seven to five against letting the anonymous donor put public restrooms on city-owned land. Faye was furiously writing away when Bill walked over and offered to buy her lunch.

"Well, thank you, Bill. You moved to the hotel yet? I heard you have your house up for sale."

"There's not much that gets by you. Is there any more gossip I need to hear? Who do you think our secret donor is?"

"So far, I've only got intuition to stand on. I think the person has lived here his whole life, has some money, and wants to spend it on the town rather than squander it on ungrateful relatives. You might say he's listing us as his heirs and giving us our share while he's still here to see it being used."

At the Ritz Hotel Bistro, Bill asked the waiter if Andre had anything special on the day's menu. He was told they were featuring a pork loin wrapped in peppered bacon and glazed with pineapple. It was served with new potatoes swimming in melted butter and french-cut green beans.

"Hello, Willie. May I join you?" Harriet had been shuffled to the hotel two days before. She was gradually finding her way around town and decided today she would eat lunch with Bill. She'd been waiting an hour for him to show up.

"Faye, let me introduce you to my ex-wife, Harriet." He stood and pulled out a chair. "Harriet, this is Miss Faye Spencer, a reporter for the *Meteor*, and a very close friend."

The two women shook hands.

Harriet said, "Honey, I'm still Mrs. Potter."

"Harriet, you left me twenty years ago. This is the first time you've been back. I'm going to have those papers drawn up this afternoon."

"Okay, but I want the hotel."

They ordered the lunch special and entered into polite conversation while Bill began to sweat under the collar. After the meal, Faye excused herself saying she had to get back to the paper and write her article on the city council meeting.

"Can I walk you back?" Bill asked.

"No. You stay and talk with Harriet. I imagine you two have a lot to catch up on. And some things to iron out."

Bill watched Faye walk to the door. She was sure a good-looking woman. She must be six feet tall. Such a magnificent woman. Red hair, long legs, beautiful green eyes. Bill's face was one big smile. Someone rushed to open the door for Faye.

"My, my, Bill. Have we got a relationship here?"

"Harriet, I think you've let the air out of my balloon."

CHAPTER 3—THE PLAYERS

February 8, 1945 (nine days before the double murder)

"Gin. Let's see, that makes two hundred seventy-five dollars. You gonna call your dad for the money or will I be taking it outta your hide?"

"Damnit, Gleason. You know I'm good for it. I've never seen a man with so much luck."

Gleason Bonds stuffed his cards in their cardboard box. He'd only been playing with his new cellie for a month but the stakes had escalated and now he'd get all the boy's cigarette money. He had a mirror on the metal shelf. There was no way he'd lose but maybe he'd better pace himself; win slowly over a period of time and not kill the cash cow.

"Dan, your dad sends you twenty dollars every month. As long as you give it to me I'll let the rest ride until you can win it back."

Daniel got up from the only chair in their cell and climbed into his top bunk. He'd been in prison for almost seven years. In a few months he'd be reviewed for parole. He might be gone before his gambling debt ever got paid. But he didn't want to give up his cigarette money in the meantime.

"Gleason, you've bested me at gin, poker, and dominoes. I don't think I've ever won a hand at anything. Yesterday, I wrote my dad to send me a set of checkers. I think I'll hold off any more gambling until it comes. In the meantime, you can have the ten in my account. It's all I have left this month."

Over the speakerphone on the back wall came static as a pencil head bounced off a microphone. "Bonds, you got a visitor. Proceed to Admin immediately."

Gleason had two brothers. Terrell was dead so it must be Evan. His dad ignored him—acted like he'd been killed with Terrell. No one other than Evan cared whether he was dead or alive. He didn't have any friends.

Gleason arrived at Admin and was escorted through to where the visitors had to register and wait for the inmate they were visiting to be brought up. Gleason was able to talk to any visitor he might receive through a screened partition. The guards were on hand to make sure nothing was passed from one side to the other but otherwise stayed at a distance.

"Hey, bro. Got your letter. How you making it?"

"Evan, did you bring me any money? You can't get nothing done here unless you pay for it. The food's bad, the laundry stinks, even our mail's messed up unless you slip a few dollars to the man in charge."

"The guards?" Evan thought about how their dad had always been in law enforcement. He walked straight. He'd never be bribed. None of his boys had measured up.

"No. Not the guards. The inmates. If you slip a few dollars a month to the kitchen help you find the food you get's actually edible. A few more dollars to the laundry guys and your clothes come back clean and dry. A few dollars to the men in the mail room and your letters get posted or delivered. If you don't pay you live like an animal."

"I'll talk to dad."

"Listen, Evan. I know of a woman with ten thousand dollars stashed away. It's money from a robbery. The guy's doing a fifteen-year stint and she's holding it for him. I got her address and name from a letter I found. He'll be getting out before me so you got to go get that money. You can put my share in my account monthly."

"Wow. Ten big ones. How should I do it? I mean, do you know where she keeps it? What do you know about her?"

"Relax, Evan, she lives alone and has it hidden somewhere in her apartment. Just keep a lookout and when she leaves you ransack the place. If you can't find it, put a mask over your face and be standing behind the door when she returns. She'll give it to you."

Leaving the Ritz Hotel Bistro Faye walked briskly toward the newspaper's office. The wind had picked up so she buttoned her coat and increased her pace. It was only a few blocks. When she got to her destination she noticed a bum standing in an alleyway across the street. He turned when she looked in his direction.

All afternoon she wrestled with who the secret donor might be. She wrote the article about the city council meeting and filed her notes. He was still there, the man in the alleyway. Maybe she should leave out the back. That's ridiculous. This is Dancing Deer. Nothing happens here. It's five o'clock. Time to call it a day. She had to get back to the apartment and Katy.

Faye put on her coat. From her pockets she retrieved a pair of mittens and a stocking cap. The weather had deteriorated since lunch. Opening the door Faye stepped into the chill. The bum lunged from the alleyway, heading in her direction. She took a step, looked at him again, and went back inside the newspaper office. She found Jesse loitering around the break room. He was also getting ready to leave.

"Jesse, Katy's abusive husband is here. He's seen me."

The front door flew open and in walked the bum. No one was there except the receptionist, Faye, and Jesse. Galen walked past the receptionist. Jesse and Faye came out of the break room and came face to face with the man Faye feared more than any other man in this world.

"Faye, aren't you glad to see me?"

"Galen, get out of here. I don't want to see you. I don't want to have anything to do with you."

Grabbing Faye's arm, Galen said, "Where's Katy? You tell me where I can find my lovely wife and I'll not bother you anymore."

Jesse got in Galen's face. "Mister, if the lady says she doesn't want to have anything to do with you then you best leave."

"Oh, and what might you do, little man?"

Jesse grabbed Galen's arm, wrenching it from clutching Faye. Galen hit Jesse in the face. Jesse didn't see it coming. He'd never been a fighter. He fell against the wall. Galen hit him again as he slid to the floor. Jesse lost consciousness after a foot came crashing into the side of his face, jerking his head to one side. Blood spewed from his nose and mouth.

The receptionist called the police when Faye ran into her office, locking the door. Galen walked over. "I'm not leaving without Katy . . . unless I've got that money." He stormed out five minutes before the police arrived.

Faye helped Jesse sit up. She got a wet towel from the break room and wiped the blood from his face. She used another towel wrapped around ice chips to press against his nose and lips. Everything was starting to swell. One eye was already closed.

Through thick lips Jesse said, "Call Genevieve. Tell her I'll be late getting home. Then call Herman Eberly and tell him I'm coming by. If he's not at his store call him at his home. That number is on a pad in my center desk drawer."

Jesse tried to get to his feet when Faye went to the telephone. Unsteady and with a big knot on the side of his head, he felt flushed, about to faint. He made it to a chair and waited for Faye to return.

"He'll be there for another hour."

"Good. Let's take my picture. If anything comes of this I want proof of my injuries."

Later, after the police left with a description of Galen Hamelin and a promise from Jesse to come to police headquarters for a statement, Faye drove Jesse to Eberly's Sporting Goods.

"Damn, Jesse. What happened to you?"

"I got decked by Faye's brother-in-law. He's nothing but trouble. I need a gun in case he comes after me again."

"Oh, man. You sure you want a gun? By the way you look, a bazooka might be more in order."

"Very funny. A gun and a couple of boxes of ammunition. I've got to learn how to shoot the thing."

"Okay. I wouldn't recommend anything in the larger calibers. They're so much heavier they're hard to aim and so much bigger they're hard to conceal. Probably a .38 police special. Here, how does this feel?"

"Awkward."

"Maybe you'd like an automatic instead. I have a Beretta that shoots a 9 mm. It's a lot more expensive but a real quality piece of workmanship."

"Yeah. This is good. I'll take it. You got any shoulder holsters?"

"Only by special order. Let me get my catalogs."

Fifteen minutes later Jesse had purchased an equalizer and ordered a place to put it. He wrote Herman a check and stuffed the gun and ammo in his pocket. He was starting to feel better and drove Faye to the police station to swear out a complaint.

Afterwards he took Faye to her apartment and headed on to his house. He dreaded explaining what had happened to Genevieve. She'd get her purse and go after Galen herself if Jesse didn't word it just right.

On the way to his house in the country Jesse drove past Snockered. Galen was walking up to the front door. Venom spread through Jesse's body. He parked and walked inside. Galen was already playing pool on the back table with a couple of rough-looking characters. Jesse picked up a pool cue. Galen concentrated on making a combination shot, pocketing the nine-ball in a side pocket. Jesse walked straight for Galen. He brought the pool cue down on Galen's head just as Galen stroked the cue ball, sending it on its way. No one would ever know if the nine ball would drop because when Jesse came down with the pool cue, Galen's head smashed against several balls caroming around the table.

Galen slithered to the floor. Dazed, he looked up at Jesse holding a broken pool cue with the jagged end pressed against his wind pipe.

"If you so much as set foot in my newspaper office again or if I hear of you bothering any of my employees, I'll come looking for you with a gun. You got that?"

Jesse threw down the broken cue and made his way out through the throng of onlookers. No one hindered his way. They all knew who he was and no one knew anything about the bum lying on the floor. Jesse put a sawbuck on the till and stepped out into the night feeling much better.

"Jesse, darling, what happened?" Genevieve helped Jesse take off his jacket.

"My first fight. You remember me telling you about Faye's sister coming down to visit from Kansas City, well, it seems it wasn't just a friendly visit. She was escaping from an abusive husband. He's now followed her here and located Faye. I told him to leave and he showed me how the cow ate the cabbage."

Genevieve hung up Jesse's coat while he went to the bathroom to wash his hands. Margaret walked over from her sitting room and asked when dinner would be ready. "Son, did you get kicked by a horse?"

"No, Mother. One of the plates of typeset fell on me and I was knocked into the press while it was running. I'll be all right. I'll chalk it up to gaining experience."

"My goodness, what a lot of swelling. How come there's no ink? I would think falling into a running newspaper press you'd be black with ink."

"I washed it off."

"What a lot of improvements I've seen. Used to that ink stayed on for days. And now you can just wash it off. My goodness. Son, is it a new kind of ink?"

"Mom, I really don't want to talk any more about it."

Walking into the kitchen Genevieve whispered into her husband's ear, "Nor dig any deeper into a growing quagmire of lies."

Jesse's father passed away last December and then in January, after a whirlwind romance, Jesse and Genevieve were married. Margaret, Jesse's mother, begged Jesse and Genevieve to live with her. She told them how lonely she was now that Mr. Bell was gone. She didn't know what she'd do in her big old house by herself. She said she wouldn't be any trouble.

They had Rupert Calhoun, a local carpenter, link two adjacent upstairs bedrooms with a wide opening and added a bathroom. She had her own apartment within what was now Jesse's house. Genevieve would have preferred their own place but Margaret really did keep to herself. She proved to be decent companionship those times when Genevieve wanted it; she did her own thing at other times.

Jesse's house was at the end of the line and the next day Genevieve caught a city bus into downtown. She walked into Eberly's Sporting Goods and told Herman she needed a box of .45 caliber pistol cartridges.

"What kind of gun you plan on firing them from?"

"It's an FP-45 Liberator."

"Like the ones we dropped into France when it was under German occupation?"

"Yes. One of them."

"Do you have it with you? I've never actually seen one. Just pictures."

A few minutes later the transaction was completed, the store proprietor impressed, and the gun back in Genevieve's purse. No one would have to know, unless she had occasion to use it. Jesse was such a gentle soul. He was too much a gentleman to handle a thug like Katy's husband. He'd need somebody to look out for him. Someone to make sure he was safe.

Faye needed help. As soon as she arrived at her apartment and told Katy about Galen, she called her neighbor, Sheriff Sherman Shodtoe. He said he'd be right over.

To Katy she said, "What's this money Galen's talking about?"

"Faye, I meant to tell you about it. When dad died he left me an inheritance. One day, out of the blue, a man in a business suit showed up at our door. At first, I was scared witless; I thought it might be one of those men Galen owed all that money to. But he shoved a business card under the door saying he was a lawyer. On the back he had penciled in 'Hardy estate $50,000.' When I let him in he told me he was Dad's lawyer and he'd been trying to find me for months. I had him cash in all the stocks and bonds. He gave me a sizable amount of cash and a cashier's check for the remainder.

"Faye, I've never had any money in my life and now I'm a rich woman. Galen wouldn't even give me local bus money. He was afraid I'd leave him so he kept me penniless and penned up like a criminal. I took the money and ran."

"He's found you now and he knows about the money. Let's not compound our problems by telling anyone else. You keep that money safe and secret until we can open a bank account and get it safely deposited."

"I bet he found that card. Faye, he'll kill to get my money. We've been running from those boys in Chicago and, if he can get his hands on it, he'll use it to pay them off. But it won't matter, in a few more months he'll be back in the same pile of dung. I took his gun when I left. I thought I would be better off with it. I didn't want him tracking me down with a gun in his pocket."

"Let me see it," said Faye.

Katy was gone for a few minutes and came back with a paper sack. Inside was a blued Colt .45 automatic.

"Did you bring any bullets?"

"No. But I think it's already loaded."

A knock on the door. The sheriff had arrived. Katy put her gun away while Faye answered the door.

"Sherman, thank you for coming. I don't know what to do. Jesse's been beat-up and Katy's scared out of her mind."

"Whoa. Calm down, baby. Daddy's here. Now, who beat up Jesse and who's Katy?"

Faye took the sheriff's hand and led him into the front room. Katy emerged from the bedroom.

"Sherman, this is my sister, Katy Hamelin. Katy, this is the Marsden County Sheriff, Sherman Shodtoe."

"Good looks must run in the family," said the toady sheriff.

"Katy's my step-sister. We had different fathers." Faye sat down in a chair leaving the sofa for the sheriff and her sister. "Katy's husband's been running from some people in Chicago. Last year he dragged Katy to Kansas City to hide out. He wouldn't let her out of his sight. Not for a minute. The man's a beast. Katy got fed up and when her chance came she ran away to come live with me. Now, he's here. He tried to make me tell him where she was. At the newspaper office he grabbed my arm and Jesse stepped between us. The brute almost killed Jesse, then ran out saying he would take her back or else."

"Mrs. Hamelin, why's your husband running?"

"He's a gambler and owes the Canneli brothers a lot of money."

"Is that Canneli as in Canneli Import Company?"

Katy nodded.

"I don't think you have anything to worry about. I live across the street and my cousin works for the police department. I'll get him to have an officer keep an eye on your place. Between the two of us you'll receive all the protection you can tolerate. In the meantime, you ladies got anything to drink?"

Sherman Shodtoe had always liked guns. He also liked telling people what to do. He thought he was important in some way and wanted other people to know it as well. He was a natural law enforcement candidate. Trouble was he had no proper training. To be county sheriff you had to be elected. Knowing proper police procedures and tactics were secondary to being in the right place at the right time and having the right endorsement.

When the incumbent sheriff retired, Sherman offered to hire his son as a deputy if the sheriff would endorse him. Having a deadbeat son is nothing to brag about. The sheriff thought that if getting his son a good job only required a few kind words then they would be well spent. The sheriff was a Democrat with Sherman being a registered Republican. Sherman had outflanked his opposition and ran unopposed. Two weeks later he told the departing sheriff he couldn't hire his son for a year or so. Any earlier and it would look like he had bought the endorsement. He never did hire the deadbeat kid.

As soon as he was elected he started cleaning house. The county allowed him four dispatchers: one for the day shift, another for the evening shift, and two part-timers for Friday through Sunday. He also was allowed two deputies. He hired two childhood friends to be the principal dispatchers. There was a constant round-robin of people for work at the end of the week. For the deputies he hired his twin nephews.

Rafe and Ralph Johnson were identical. Even their mother had a hard time distinguishing them. Sherman didn't try. On the radio they were called by their squad car number. When they were together he referred to them as boys and individually as Johnson. Growing up, they occasionally switched identities. In an effort to tell them apart the teachers made them attend different classes. That played right into the boys' hands. They always wore identical clothing, combed their hair the same way, and developed the same mannerisms. After the first took a test, they'd meet at the shared locker. The first one quickly looked through his textbook and, changing places with his brother, took the test again. For variety they even traded girlfriends. No one was the wiser and both boys thought their little game hilarious.

Sherman didn't score well with the ladies. He had a brusque way of talking, using short contrite sentences full of simple words and little substance. He didn't come across as someone worth listening to. Most people took his position into consideration and avoided lengthy conversation. Others considered him intellectually inferior and talked to him in a condescending manner. They were put on his mental list. He was continually checking his list and retaliating against anyone on it at every possible opportunity.

When he asked Faye Spencer if she would go to dinner and listen to the big band of Baxter Black at the Ritz Grand Hotel and Ballroom he was surprised when she accepted. It took half a week's pay to buy the tickets and pay for their meal. And she spent most of her time dancing with that Calhoun carpenter and talking to Bill Potter. He fumed. Every time after that, she had other plans when he called. She probably thought she could do better. She was now on his list as well as Claude Calhoun and Bill Potter.

He told his deputies to find out what they could about the new members on his list. Faye Spencer, as it turned out, didn't have any skeletons in her closet. Claude Calhoun lived in Fort Smith over eighty miles away. Bill Potter, on the other hand, lived in Dancing Deer and was immersed in less than honorable activities. One of them involved Sherman's attractive neighbor, Raylene. She lived across the street on the floor below Faye Spencer and on the backside of the building. The other tenants being senior citizens made him think the men walking around the building to enter from the back door had to be visiting Raylene. The sheriff soon determined that Bill spent every Friday night at Raylene's apartment. They were never together in mixed company. No one was even aware they had a relationship.

Sherman bought a telescope and started keeping an eye on Faye's apartment and the secretive men. They came and went on a regular schedule. He decided Raylene must be operating a one-woman brothel.

One Thursday evening he paid a visit. "Hello, Miss Carlisle. I'm Sheriff Sherman Shodtoe."

"Yes, I've seen you around. What can I do for you, Sheriff?" asked Raylene.

"There have been some complaints about strange men lurking outside your apartment. I've been keeping an open eye and it appears the same men visit you on Monday, Wednesday, and Friday nights. Do you have any comments?"

"Yes I do, Sheriff. You're county. You have no probable cause to stalk me. Your duties are to deliver papers from the county court and keep the peace county wide. Let's call Police Chief Wainwright and see what business you might have harassing law-abiding citizens in his town."

"There's no need to do that. Just be aware that what you do and what you sell have been noticed. Now if you would like to offer those same services in return for special favors I would be the first to counter with my gratitude. I'd tell my boys your business is private."

"Sheriff, my favors are my private business. You don't scare me. I wouldn't let a cretin like you pet my dog much less share my bed." She slammed the door shut and went and called W.W. to see if he might like a free night.

Sheriff Sherman Shodtoe put Raylene's name at the top of his list.

Katy was worried sick. The police officer sat in an unmarked patrol car across the street. She kept an eye on him hoping it would be twenty-four hour surveillance. Occasionally, he started the engine, probably, to get the heater going. Smoke came out of the tailpipe and announced his presence to anyone walking by. Twice she had gone down and delivered a large cup of steaming coffee. One time she took him a blanket but he still kept warm by running the engine.

When Faye came home from work she plopped down a box of .45 caliber cartridges. "You might not hit what you're aiming at with the first shot. If I was you I'd put a handful of bullets in a sack and keep them and the gun in my purse. Then I'd keep that purse with me everywhere I went. Do you know if there's a safety?"

"No. I just thought I'd point and shoot."

"Go get it and let's see how it works."

The next hour they fiddled with the gun. They figured out how to remove the clip, how to insert new cartridges, how to re-insert the clip, and how to load the first round. What they didn't know was how much effort was necessary to actually pull the trigger. Katy held the gun up, looking down its sights.

"This thing is so heavy it takes two hands to hold. Why do you think he needed such a big gun?"

Katy removed the clip, removed the cartridges, and shoved home the empty cartridge housing. She then pulled the trigger. There was a blast. The window shattered, with the bullet ricocheting off the brick of the building across the street and through the windshield of the unmarked patrol car. The two girls ran to the window. On the sidewalk a man was looking up. The door of the car opened and the police officer jumped out with his gun in hand and dashed across the street into their building.

Katy set the gun down on the kitchen counter and went to the door. The officer bounded up three flights of stairs and when he came to the third floor landing, he held his gun in both hands pointing in her direction.

"I'm sorry, Officer. It went off by accident."

The officer lowered his gun a bit and hesitantly walked her way. Reaching the doorway, he pushed her aside, raised his gun, and surveyed the interior of the apartment. "You fired at me by mistake?"

"I didn't fire at you. I was checking a gun I thought was unloaded. I wanted to see how much pressure was needed to pull the trigger and it went off, blowing out the window. I'm sorry. You weren't hit were you?"

"No, but the windshield and driver's side window are busted."

"Here, Officer. Sit down." She turned to Faye and said, "Fix this man something to drink. I'll go down and shut his car door." To the policeman she asked, "Have you had supper?"

Later he had to write up a report and take his car into the city garage to get new glass installed. Those two crazy women shouldn't mess around with guns. Hell, they shouldn't be allowed to cook.

The next day Katy went to the police station to make arrangements to reimburse the city for the damage and to pay the fine for firing a gun in the city limits. She sat at an officer's desk and asked if anyone was looking for her husband. She was informed that Jesse had dropped his charge of assault and battery and, since her husband had done nothing illegal, they had no reason to look for him. They were also removing the officer from the street in front of her apartment.

"What about my safety? The man's going to kill me."

"You can get a restraining order. Then if he shows up we can arrest him."

"Okay, that's a start."

CHAPTER 4—PEPE
February 15, 1945 (The day before the double murder)

Pepe didn't speak English. He came from France with his daughter when she was chasing after David Calhoun. David saved them both and their town's bell from the Germans. Genevieve shot David in the struggle, then nursed him back to health. When Pepe used his son's racing car to take David back to his unit he had no idea that a few months later David would be wounded and sent home a hero.

When Genevieve found out David had been shot, Pepe had to take her to him—all the way to Dancing Deer. But their relationship was not to be. David loved another. Then Genevieve met David's best friend, Jesse. Two months later they were married and he was now waiting to see how long it would take for Genevieve to get pregnant.

Pepe thought Dancing Deer was a beautiful town but was eager to see the rest of America. He shouldn't have to wait much longer: Genevieve was a beautiful woman in the flower of youth and Jesse was a lusty young man. Maybe a little too smart, a little too involved with his newspaper, a little too involved with his community, but Genevieve could take care of that.

As soon as Genevieve told him she was with child Pepe would check out of the hotel and see the rest of the country. He'd return in time to see the baby born, then head home to France. Pepe had his foreman bringing the Martel vineyard back and he wanted to be there to offer his views on the matter.

Pepe had his menu. He kept it in his back pocket. Genevieve had overwritten in French what the menu said in English. All he had to do was point, but that took the hand not holding the menu and he didn't want to disturb that hand. He and the waitress had a thing going. With his hand hanging over the edge of the table it had lately been her custom to lean up against it. Sometimes she was facing forward and sometimes she backed up. Pepe's mouth watered. He ate all of his meals there, taking an extremely long time to actually place an order. When he became aroused to the point of gasping he'd been asking for "the special" and waited with glassy eyes to see what the chef would surprise him with. Today there was a new waitress and things were not going smoothly.

In French, someone said, "Monsieur, may I be of assistance?" Harriet was standing beside the waitress. She had learned to speak French in school and spent two summers in Paris before meeting her Willie.

"Mademoiselle, I would be honored. Besides my daughter, you and I are the only ones in Arkansas who speak my beautiful language. Please, have a seat. For a bit of conversation I will supply you with wit and story."

"It's early and you, Monsieur, have already made my day. Let me help you order and then we'll descend to the depths of your wit and story. My name is Harriet Potter." She held out her hand.

Pepe took her hand in his and kissed it. "Miss Potter, my name is Henri . . . no. no. That was in another life. My name is Pepe Martel. Please, call me Pepe."

"Okay, Pepe. You may call me Harriet. But I must warn you. I'm married. However, I think my husband's filing for divorce as soon as he can figure out the least amount of aggravation he can bring on himself and the most amount of money he can stand to part with."

"Well then, Mrs. Potter . . . Harriet, will you please ask the young lady if the wonderful chef would fix me a crepe with strawberries and whipped cream?"

"That sounds delightful. I'll tell her. I might have to go into the kitchen and show him how to prepare it myself. Soon he'll be working for me anyway."

"Harriet, we should dwell within your wit. You must tell me your story. I think anything I can come up with will pale in comparison."

"You are too kind."

After their meal and for the rest of the day Pepe and Harriet went through the hotel like it was already hers. They went to the kitchen first and met Andre and his staff. Harriet made suggestions of items to add to the menu and tried to determine if they were adequately supplied with the proper spices and ingredients. Next they toured the administrative offices. She promptly told everyone that when she took over no one should be alarmed. She was not planning on making wholesale changes. She wanted to gradually take over and slowly mold their operation to her own personality. They then went to the laundry facilities. Harriet introduced herself to the maids, to the maintenance men, and to the concierge at his station near the front door.

She began to think this was going to be a marvelous improvement. Her social life in Boston had become tedious. This was the adventure she'd been looking for.

Pepe thought, with Faye Spencer not able to speak French and the waitress younger than his daughter, Harriet might be the woman he'd been looking for.

CHAPTER 5—SNOCKERED
February 16, 1945 (hours before the double murder)

It was Friday. Bill had a standing appointment for Fridays at Raylene's. Tonight he would end the relationship. She lived in the same apartment building as Faye. If he continued he would eventually get caught. If he really wanted his relationship with Faye to grow, his relationship with Raylene would have to end. Bill needed a drink.

Just outside the city limits was the town honky-tonk and pool hall. Snockered was run by Big Bear Radisson. Bear was also the bartender and owner. He had come to the bank soon after they passed the county ordinance allowing liquor by the drink for established clubs. Bear wanted to open a pool hall and serve alcohol. Bill decided this type of business was inevitable with the new ordinance but if he handled it just right the city wouldn't have to suffer the degenerates it spawned. Bill offered to loan the money if it would be located outside the city limits. Since then, Bill went out there once a month to check on his customer, have a few drinks, and play a few racks of snooker.

Bill sat on a stool at the bar. He had a sad look on his face. Raylene had been his main squeeze for the last ten years. Although they were never seen together in public he had become attached to her in a profound way.

Raylene spent a lot of time preparing for his evening. At the start of their relationship she successfully figured out what his sexual fantasies were and proceeded to provide what he had only dreamed about. She started to enter his thoughts around Monday and they increased in intensity until Friday afternoon, when he couldn't stand it any longer. He'd burst into her apartment wanting immediate gratification. She toyed with him, made him eat a meal, listen to records or the radio, and whatever else she could think of to heighten the pleasure he would soon have. Afterwards, they slept nestled snug against each other until the morning sun stole through the window.

"What'll you have, Mr. Potter?" Bear stood in front of Bill with a rag stuck in his apron. Bear was six foot seven and at three hundred plus pounds he was the biggest man in Dancing Deer. Big Bear Radisson didn't put up with any crap. He ran a tight ship. County deputy, Rafe or Ralph, came in on weekends to accentuate the point. Bear couldn't tell the two twins apart and couldn't care less. They didn't have to do anything, just be there. Sometimes they sat in their patrol car and sometimes in a back booth. Sometimes gone for a hour or so, then back walking through the tables. Between a deputy sheriff and Bear there was no patron with enough nerve to get in the least bit of trouble.

"Vodka, neat—double—from your freezer."

"You planning on doing some serious drinking, Mr. Potter?"

"You might say, Bear. I've got a serious problem to solve."

Bill was into his third drink when he asked for his pool cue and the balls for the snooker table. The eight-ball tables were coin-operated and busy. Several coins lined up next to the slot for each from people waiting their turn. Not many of Bear's patrons played snooker. It was not as much a hustler's game and took a lot more skill. The table was larger at five by ten, the rails firmer, and the pockets and balls smaller. Luck didn't play a large role in snooker. It took a steady eye, a light stick, a knowledge of angles, and a plan of strategy. Bill racked the red balls and placed the numbered balls on their spots.

"Want a game?" Bill looked up to a tall, rough-looking man with a cap pulled to the front and snapped to the bill. He had a cue in his hand and was rubbing green chalk on its tip.

"Sure. But, I've only got an hour."

"Wanna play for a dollar a point?"

"Okay. You a hustler?"

"Yeah. Name's Galen Hamelin." Galen held out his hand.

"Bill Sucker Potter."

They shook hands. After the first game and two more drinks, Bill was up by twenty-five dollars and Galen had started sweating. On the second game, Bill broke with the red balls caroming all around the table but nothing falling. Galen held a cube of green chalk in his bridge hand and ran a smooth twenty-seven points, leaving the cue ball resting against the five. Bill miscued and Galen ran off another thirty points.

When it was Bill's time to shoot he rubbed his hand on a hard pyramid of caked powder, slapped it onto the lower part of his cue, and chalked the tip. Bill pocketed a red ball, the five, another red ball, the five, another red ball, and prepared to shoot at the five a third time. Galen was standing directly behind Bill and when Bill made his final preliminary stroke prior to hitting the cue ball, Galen lightly touched the rubber end of Bill's cue, causing Bill to stroke a little off line and miss the five altogether, scratching. Bill looked behind to see what he'd hit but Galen had already moved around the table to take his next shot. Bill entered his six points and noticed Galen had three runs instead of the two he remembered.

"Hold on. I think we need some supervision here. You got three runs listed but only two are correct. And you bumped me on my last shot."

Galen chalked the end of his cue. "Mister, you calling me a cheat?"

"What I'm saying is that last run you entered for twenty-two points has to come off and I get to continue shooting with you standing away from the table."

"I don't see it that way."

"It doesn't matter what way you see it. If you want to continue playing for money then that's what's required."

"Okay. Don't get your dander up." Galen went over to the board erased his last run and handed Bill the cue ball. "How about we make it five dollars a point."

"You're on, but Bear keeps score."

"Okay, Bear keeps score. Let's start a new rack. Bear, give my buddy here another drink." Bill broke with three red balls falling. Next he shot the five, hitting the cue ball below center making it back up six inches and stop after striking the object ball. Snooker was a game of position. He ran twenty-two points before missing a bank shot in the side pocket.

"Man, you like them side pockets."

Galen ran two red balls, the seven, and the four before leaving Bill snookered behind the two. Bill shot the cue ball away from the two into the corner where it hit two rails, bounded out, and hit a lonely red ball, then came to rest against a rail. Galen ran seventeen points, leaving

Bill snookered again, this time three inches behind the four with all the red balls on the other end of the table. Bill shot a *masse* shot. With his cue almost vertical Bill stroked down on the side of the cue ball with a quick jerk. The ball, spinning furiously, curved around the four to hit a red ball and pocketing it in the corner. Bill then proceeded to run eighteen points. Galen scored twelve points, leaving Bill corner-hooked. Bill scratched and Galen scored another twenty points before missing a combination. Bill then ran the table amassing an astounding forty-five points. Bill unscrewed his pool cue and placed it in its leather box. He had one more drink while Bear calculated with a head of steam. It took Bear several minutes before he pointed to Galen.

"On the first two games, you won by thirty-three points. At a dollar a ball, you won thirty-three dollars. This last game, Mr. Potter won by sixteen points. At five dollars a point, he wins eighty dollars. Mister, you owe Bill forty-seven dollars."

Galen reached into a pocket and pulled out his wad of bills. He counted it but only had thirty dollars. He handed Bill all his money and said, "I'll have to pay you the rest tomorrow. Give me your address and I'll bring it by."

Bill took the money and said, "That's all right. I'll take this and we'll call it even. Bear give the man a drink on me. I think he's about to leave."

Galen gulped down the drink and walked outside. He'd hide in the dark and wait on Mister Potter. In the next few minutes Bill drank another vodka, gave Bear his cue, paid his tab, and left. He needed to go to Raylene's while he still had his mind made up. Seeing Galen lurking behind an evergreen, Bill reached into his pocket for his billfold and took out five twenties.

"Mr. Hamelin. You play a good stick; best game I've had in years. Here's a hundred dollars. Don't get yourself into any more trouble. In that car over there facing the front door and idling is Ralph, or maybe Rafe, a county deputy. He'd like nothing better than for you to cause a little trouble."

Galen snatched the money. "We'll play again some day. Maybe you won't be so damned lucky." Galen walked back into the bar.

Rafe called the dispatcher. He'd found Galen Hamelin.

CHAPTER 6—THE WARRANT

February 17, 1945 (the day after the murders)

Bill stood on a stool looking at the shelf above his hanging clothes. What did he have up there? He got everything down and put them into three piles: those items he'd move to his new residence, those donated to charity, and those trashed. The first pile was by far the smallest with the third the largest. The doorbell rang.

"Good morning, Chief. What gets you out this early on a Saturday?"

"Bill, can I come in? I've got some bad news." W.W. Wainwright had his hat in his hands.

"Sure, come on in. Has anything happened to Rose?" The chief shook his head. "Carson?"

"No. Bill, were you at Raylene's house last night?"

"Yeah. How'd you know?"

"Someone saw you run to your car."

"Well, I wasn't exactly running. It was cold . . . and windy."

"What were you doing there?"

"I . . . uh, I . . . Raylene's a customer at the bank . . ."

"Bill, were you one of Raylene's paying customers?"

Bill sat down. "Yeah, I guess I was."

"Was?"

"Last night I told her I needed to break off our relationship. My ex-wife has come back and complicated things. Also, I've become interested in another woman and I didn't want her finding out what I did on Friday evenings."

"What did Raylene have to say?"

"She was upset. She had planned this elaborate meal and bought some 78's for us to listen to. She said she didn't know how she'd pay for her apartment. I've been paying her rent for the last ten years."

"You've been seeing Raylene for ten years?"

51

"Yeah. She grows on you. I've never met a more confusing woman. I used to think I loved her but when pressured she assured me it was only business. She made my entire week in that one Friday night. But I had to call it off. I need someone all the time. I think this new woman is the one. I've just got to convince her and not screw things up."

"Someone killed Raylene last night."

"No." Bill jumped from his seat. "How could that happen? No one was supposed to be there but me. I was her Friday."

"We don't know yet. There was also a man killed in front of her apartment building—shot in the head. Bill, I've got a search warrant for your house and the Packard." He pulled out a legal document from the breast pocket of his jacket and handed it to a stunned Bill.

Bill read the first couple of paragraphs. "It says you're looking for a gun, a shoe, a pillow, and an address book. I've got lots of shoes and pillows but no guns. I've always been afraid of guns and Raylene wouldn't let anyone see her address book."

"If she was dead she couldn't stop anyone."

"Look all you want. I didn't kill Raylene. I'm a changed man."

"You mean you used to kill people but you've now quit?"

"No. I just started looking at things differently. I was a ruthless businessman but finally came to my senses and have been trying to be a better citizen and a better father."

"I hope you're right. My gut says you didn't kill Raylene but you might've killed that creep on her sidewalk." The chief surveyed the area. "What's all the piles on the floor for?"

"I've decided to move to the hotel. I've just started to get things sorted into what gets moved and what doesn't."

"Have you moved anything yet?"

"No, but I've got a dozen bags in the garage I was planning on leaving by the curb for Monday's pickup."

Chief Wainwright went to the front door and motioned for the two men in a second patrol car to come inside. "Bill, you got any coffee?"

Bill held his head in his hands. Raylene was dead. "Could that man outside have killed her?"

"I don't know. We haven't found the gun. Raylene's body has some slight bruising, but we're not sure how she died. The coroner's doing an autopsy."

One of the two police officers started rummaging through Bill's bedroom. The second officer went to the garage through a door in the kitchen. In a few minutes he came back.

"Chief, I found a gun in Mr. Potter's car." He walked into the living room dangling a .38 snub-nosed Smith and Wesson Police Special from a pencil stuck behind the trigger.

"Good work Henderson, but you're supposed to be working with Officer McRae. I want the two of you working together, not individually. Bill, this your gun?"

"Hell, no. I don't own a gun." Bill turned to the officer holding the gun. "You say you found that in my car?"

"In the glove box."

"You, sir, are a liar."

"Bill, if this proves to be the murder weapon you're going to need a good lawyer. I'd advise you against making any statements without him present. This afternoon you need to come by the station and have your fingerprints taken."

"Is that necessary?" asked Bill.

"If that gun has your fingerprints on it then you'll have a hard time denying having knowledge of it. If, on the other hand, it doesn't have your fingerprints then it'll give a lot of credibility to your protestations."

There was a loud clanging noise. "Ow. Damnit."

The chief, Bill, and the officer holding the gun hurried to where the noise came from. The chief said, "What's going on, McRae?"

"I was looking in the coat pockets and this wooden box fell off the shelf and hit me on the head." He reached over and opened the box. It was full of shoe polish, buffing brushes, and extra shoelaces.

"Be more careful, McRae. We don't want to damage any of Mr. Potter's things. Find that address book."

The chief looked at Bill. "You better hope we don't find that book."

By noon the search was winding down with the only other mishap happening to Officer Henderson. He received an electrical shock turning on the light in Rose's bedroom. They took the gun and a right shoe from every pair of dress shoes Bill owned. The book and the pillow remained missing.

CHAPTER 7—THE DISTRICT ATTORNEY
February 19, 1945

"Chief, what we got here?"

"Two murders without anything linking them together, except one was inside an apartment on the second floor and one outside on the sidewalk."

The district attorney retrieved a pad of paper from his desk. "Who are our suspects?"

"Raylene Carlisle was a woman who sold sexual favors to a few well-to-do Dancing Deer citizens. Bill Potter had been seeing her for ten years. The apartment was in his name. He said Friday was his night and he'd terminated their relationship that night leaving around ten. We have a witness but she didn't see his face. She did see his car—a black Packard Sedan. Bill doesn't deny being there but says Raylene was only a little agitated when he left. He went in the back, as always, but left through the front."

"How was she killed?"

"The coroner says she was smothered with a pillow. The killer must have taken it with him, as one is missing."

"Any fingerprints?"

"Yeah, lots. But none belong to the man outside. We haven't been able to identify any others—except Potter."

"Still haven't found the address book?"

"No, sir, and none of Bill's shoes had traces of blood."

"Okay. What about the man outside?"

"He's been identified as Galen Hamelin. His wife, Katy, ran off to hide with her sister, Faye Spencer. Hamelin tracked Katy down. She claims he had with ties to organized crime in Chicago. Also, he resembles the drawing of a robbery suspect in Mountain Home. One of my officers is headed up there with some pictures to see if he's their man."

"You got any suspects for his murderer?"

"Yeah. He'd been in several squabbles just the few days he's been here. He punched Jesse Bell's lights out at the newspaper office, man-handled Faye Spencer, and robbed Bill Potter. Although Bill says he gave him the money."

"Not likely, but there's a link."

"Yeah and it was on the night of the murder. According to Bear Radisson, Potter came in to get drunk. Then he got hustled at snooker by Mr. Hamelin, except Potter ended up winning all of Hamelin's money. Hamelin left with empty pockets before Potter did. A few minutes after Potter left, Hamelin came back in with a stack of twenties. Bear told him to hit the road, he wasn't welcome there anymore. We don't have any more information about his activities until he's found dead. His wife was in Faye Spencer's apartment on the front of the third floor. Miss Carlisle's apartment was on the back of the second floor."

"Were there any twenties on the body?"

"No. He didn't have any money, other than change."

"Maybe, Bill wanted his money back."

"Could be. He also could have used the money for sex, but we didn't find any in the apartment either. We did find a gun in Bill's car but don't know if it's the murder weapon. And we found a mangled .45 slug in the street but it's so damaged I don't know if we'll be able to match it with a gun. The one we found in Bill's car was a .38. It had the serial number filed off."

The district attorney had been writing everything down. "So far it looks like Bill Potter killed Hamelin. Did anyone hear Bill and Raylene argue?"

The chief didn't think Bill killed Raylene, but it wasn't his call. "No, sir, no one heard a thing. Not even a gunshot."

The district attorney put his pad down. "Hell, everyone, except those three girls, in that apartment building is old and hard of hearing. Suppose Bill comes back after he breaks up their relationship and finds Raylene in bed with Hamelin. It's his night. It's his apartment. He probably has a key. Let's say he lets himself in."

The chief interrupted, "It wouldn't take a key to get into her apartment. She didn't have a padlock, so anyone with a knife blade slipped between the door jam and the door could have gotten in."

The district attorney continued, "Raylene's in the bathroom getting ready. Bill shoots Hamelin. No. I think they've already had sex and Hamelin's asleep. Raylene's in the bathroom, or maybe the kitchen. The .38 wouldn't have much energy after going through a skull; it probably became lodged in the pillow along with the bone fragments from the back of the head. There wouldn't be much blood with a head wound. Raylene comes out of the bathroom and confronts Bill. He grabs her, bruising her neck and arm. She becomes hysterical and he puts the other pillow over her face so the neighbors won't hear. In a few minutes she's limp in his arms. He puts her on the bed, trashes the place to look like a robbery, and hauls Hamelin and the pillow toward his car. A car drives by, or maybe someone walking his dog. Bill panics, drops the body, the bone fragments fall from the pillow, and he drives off, trashing the pillow along the way."

The chief had his hand up stroking his chin. "Yeah. I see how that would work. If I could just find that pillow. But what about the footprint?"

"Well, someone called it in. Did we get a name?"

"No."

"Then the good neighbor left his footprint when he looked at the body. I think Bill's our culprit. He's got motive, opportunity, and means. Do you think our county coroner will say he thinks the gun used was a .38?"

The chief had manipulated witnesses before. "Probably. We just have to plant the idea with enough enthusiasm and make him think it was his own."

"Does Bill have an alibi?"

"No. He said he went straight home to bed. He said he was a little drunk and slept soundly until mid-morning the next day."

"Okay, Chief. Here's what we do. You comb the city for that pillow. I'll convene the Grand Jury, show probable cause, and get an indictment. Tomorrow we'll put the esteemed Bill Potter's butt in jail."

CHAPTER 8—THE INTERROGATION
February 20, 1945

It was Tuesday morning. Jellico looked over his calendar. Not much going on. A few contracts from the bank to check. Bill was buying more property. This time it was three empty lots. They weren't even next to each other. Two were on Main Street, a few blocks to the east and a few blocks to the west of the courthouse with the third two blocks south. What's he up to? The telephone rings.

"Jellico, here."

From the receiver came the familiar voice of his biggest client, Bill Potter. "Jellico, can you come down to the police station?"

"Sure. After lunch okay?"

"No, it's not. Get your lard-ass down here pronto." The telephone went silent. A dial tone pierced the silence.

"Chief, I don't want to talk to anyone without my lawyer present."

"I understand. We'll sit here and wait. Would you like something to drink? Coffee, a soda perhaps?"

"No. While you're messing around with me you're losing valuable time. The killer is still out there. You should be trying to find him."

"Bill, we think you are the killer. You had motive, opportunity, and means."

"Let's wait on Jellico."

Chief Wainwright got up from his chair at the interrogation table and left the room. It'd be a few minutes before Jellico arrived. He needed to check his messages. At his desk he took a small spiral-bound pad and flipped through its pages. The officer sent to Mountain Home had returned, saying Hamelin had been positively identified as the diner robber. Katy had identified the body found outside her sister's apartment as her husband, Galen Hamelin, and Bear Radisson had been interviewed, giving as much information as he could remember.

"Hello, Chief. Is Bill here? He called me to come down as soon as I could. We got a problem?"

"Bill has a problem. We're talking to him about the murder of Galen Hamelin and Raylene Carlisle. He wants you to be present." Chief Wainwright closed his notebook and placed it inside his vest pocket. He also turned upside-down his copy of Bear's interview.

"This is tragic. You can't possibly believe Bill is involved in any way. May I talk to him? We'll do the interview afterwards."

"One thing at a time, counselor. It's not my place to decide if Bill's implicated, that's for the state to decide. I just accumulate the evidence. Our illustrious district attorney and a grand jury will decide if the evidence is sufficient for Bill to be charged."

"Can I be assured our conversation will be private? You don't have any listening devices to turn off, do you?"

"Certainly not. He's all yours."

Jellico followed the chief into the interrogation room. Thoughts were tumbling around in his head. I'm not a criminal lawyer. Never tried a case—much less one for murder. They're not going to charge him. They just want information. And even if they did, Bill would only want my opinion of who he should hire. Whoa, this could change a boring career. Contracts, wills, estate planning, torts—just mundane stuff. Jellico thought about his picture in the Little Rock Gazette after successfully defending the notorious William Carrington Potter from a charge of murder. Hot damn!

"Jellico, they think I killed Raylene and this guy I played pool with Friday night."

"Be quiet, Bill. I'll let you know when you can talk."

For the first time in his life Bill acquiesced to the better judgment of a peer and sat down without saying a word. Jellico walked around the room trying to think of something he could use to mask their conversation. "I'll be right back."

He left the room, bumping into Chief Wainwright and his deputy Steve Trent at the door. "Chief, you got Bill sweating in there. Any chance we can get a fan?"

"Sure. Steve, get Mr. Jellico a fan. There's a plug on the leg of the table. We use it to . . . uh. I don't know what we use it for."

60

Jellico looked over Deputy Chief Steve Trent's desk while the officer went for a fan. Jellico picked up a stapler and dropped it in his overcoat pocket. Most people would feel apprehensive about stealing something from police headquarters but Jellico might have a criminal case and he was pulling out all stops. Back in the interrogation room Jellico set the fan on the rectangular table. After plugging it into the outlet on the table leg and looking under the table for any kind of mechanical eavesdropping device, he took out two business cards and folded over the ends. From his pocket he retrieved the stapler and attached the cards to the fan shroud by stapling. The electrical outlet on the chair leg didn't work so Jellico found a plug on the wall. He used his finger to whirl the blades, letting each blade slap against the cards as they turned. Bill wondered what he was doing but stayed silent as instructed.

"Bill, sit on this side of the table with your back to that window." While Bill moved, Jellico turned on the fan's power switch. The room was immediately filled with the continuous intermittent sound of flap-flap-flap. "Okay, Bill, you can talk as long as you keep it low, you're facing me, and we're sitting close to the noise."

"You think they're listening?"

"They're not supposed to and nothing you say to me can be brought up at trial but why give them any information."

Chief Wainwright and Deputy Chief Trent left the see-through mirror and went back to their desks.

"I think they're going to charge me with the murder of Raylene and a hustler I played pool with."

"What do they have?"

"That Officer Henderson planted a gun in my car and I was at Raylene's on the night of the murder. I've been paying the rent on her apartment for the last ten years."

"Were you paying for sex?"

"Yeah, a hundred dollars per month. But I decided to call off our arrangement. I was there fifteen minutes, twenty tops."

"The hundred is in addition to the rent?"

"Yep. She was worth every penny."

"And you didn't see this hustler on your way out?"

"No. I didn't see anyone."

"Okay, here's how we'll handle it. Every time they ask you a question you look at me. I'll nod if I want you to answer; otherwise, stay silent. Tell the truth if you say anything and only answer the questions asked. Don't volunteer additional information."

Jellico turned off the fan, removed his business cards, and went looking for the chief. He left the stapler on the table. At the interrogation Jellico allowed Bill to answer most of the questions asked. Bill again said he had not been robbed by Galen but had freely given him the money. No one believed him. Bill didn't give money away. Even Jellico squirmed in his seat at the obvious lie. When they had finished, Chief Wainwright produced a grand jury indictment. He said Bill would be held over, with the arraignment scheduled for the next morning at eight-thirty. Bill would spend the night in custody.

Before leaving, Jellico told Bill his charge for a murder trial would be substantially higher than his previous charges and under no circumstances was Bill to talk to anybody while in jail.

CHAPTER 9—THE ARRAIGNMENT
February 21, 1945

Bill stood before the judge in an orange jumpsuit. It was not his best day. His mouth tasted like he had dined on cotton balls. He needed a bath and a shave. Bill glanced around the room. Jellico stood at his side. Most of his friends were scattered throughout the court. On the front row sat Faye Spencer beside her boss, Jesse. Three rows back he saw his ex-wife and Rose, his daughter. On the next row farther back sat most of the Calhoun clan. He reconsidered. It was his worst day.

"Your Honor, William Carrington Potter has been indicted by the Marsden County Grand Jury and the state of Arkansas for the murder of Raylene Carlisle and Galen Hamelin."

The judge gave a stern look at Bill before turning to Michael Jellico, Bill's lawyer, and asking, "Mr. Jellico, how does Mr. Potter plead?"

"Not guilty, Your Honor."

"Does the state have a recommendation for bail?"

The lanky Emmett Irving, Marsden County District Attorney said, "Your Honor, the seriousness of the offense requires the state ask for Mr. Potter to be remanded."

"Bail is set at fifty thousand dollars—cash or bond."

"Your Honor, Bill is charged with murder."

"Yes. I am aware of that. Mr. Potter, you are not to leave the city of Dancing Deer." The judge sorted through a stack of papers. "I'll take motions next Wednesday and, if there are no objections, we'll start seating the jury the last Monday in March and commence the trial on the first Monday in April." The judge looked at the men standing by both tables, waited a moment, and slammed his gavel down, putting finality to his ruling.

Bill turned to Jellico. "Put up the deed to the Ritz. That should satisfy him."

"I'll take care of it right away. You should be out just after lunch."

"Bill, you have a visitor."

"Good, it's about time."

The jailer opened Bill's cell. "Relax. It's not Mr. Jellico. It's that newspaper lady. She wants an interview."

Bill followed the jailer to the interrogation room. "Hello, Faye. Am I going to make the front page?"

"Did you do it, Bill?"

Bill waited for the jailer to shut the door. "Faye, would you mind if I sat on that side of the table? I don't want them to be able to read my lips through the one-way glass."

Faye looked at the large mirror in the wall and moved so that their view of her would be in profile. She whispered, "Do you think they might be able to listen as well?" She cleared her throat.

"I don't know. But let me tell you and them—if they're listening. I did not do it."

"What can you tell me? The paper will have to run something across the top. A short attention grabber. Then we'll state the facts one after another. No opinion; just the facts."

"Let me think about it. We don't want people to start taking their money out of the bank. That would be disastrous. Why don't you interview my lawyer, Michael Jellico? He has all of the information and will know the wording that will hurt me the least."

"Bill, the paper is unbiased. I can't report what you want me to say. I have to report what I believe to be true. Will you be getting out anytime soon?"

"Yeah. Jellico is putting up the title to the Ritz. I should be out sometime this afternoon."

"Let's have dinner and you can fill me in on the details. In the meantime, what were you doing in Raylene's apartment?"

"Okay. I'll explain everything tonight. How about I pick you up around seven and we go to the diner out on the highway. The Ritz will be too crowded and have too many ears."

Jellico finished the paperwork and Bill stumbled out of Police Headquarters and jail at three in the afternoon. He went home to prepare for his meeting with Faye and to take a short nap. What should he tell Faye? Might as well come clean. She'll find out everything at the trial anyway. If he told her about Raylene, would she tell him to take a hike? Could he phrase it in such a way that she would not bolt from their budding romance? He had done so many things he was now ashamed of. Which ones would come out in the trial?

CHAPTER 10—THE INTERVIEW

Bill walked around the roped-off area in front of Faye's apartment building. When he got to the second floor landing he looked down the hall to Raylene's apartment and saw a yellow notice attached to her door. He hurried on to Faye's apartment one more flight up.

At the diner they got a back booth, hanging their coats on the post separating their booth from the next. Bill leaned forward. "You don't think I did it do you?"

"No, I don't. But right now you scare me. I could be wrong." Faye picked up the menu. "What are your plans?"

"I'm stepping down from running the bank and the hotel. I want the public to continue to have confidence in their management. We'll make a big deal about how I was just a figurehead anyway and they both will be better run by the management already there. In the meantime, Jellico told me to keep a low profile. These same people I'll see on the streets are going to be the ones seated in the jury box and the ones frequenting my businesses. I guess I'll catch up on my reading."

"Are you still going to move into the hotel?"

"Yes. I hired someone to move my things. They'll also be available to dispose of anything I left that Charles and Mary don't want." The waitress came by with two glasses of water and gave an appraising look before taking their orders.

"Bill, what can you tell me about your relationship with Raylene?"

Bill looked down. In a moment he said, "I've been seeing Raylene for ten years and paying for her apartment during that time. But she and I wanted different things. Her father left when she was a young girl and her mother raised her to have a cynical attitude toward men. She couldn't get close to anyone. She just used them to provide her with a comfortable lifestyle. I wasn't the only man seeing her. I'll bet every one of us would have given anything to be the only man in Raylene's life but it wasn't to be. She told me once it was just business . . . only she made it seem like so much more. Raylene was a wonderful woman. I only saw her on Friday nights but, for ten years, there was enough intimacy, enough love, enough tenderness to sustain me. I lived for that one night a week. Then I met you." Bill reached out, placing his hand over Faye's. "I told her I was ending our relationship. I wanted someone all the time—not just Friday nights. I wanted someone on my arm at the theater, someone to dance with on the Ritz ballroom floor, someone to walk with in the park, someone to kiss in the street. She said she understood, but that someone was not her—could not be her. We parted, both teary-eyed."

"What about Galen?"

"Before I went to Raylene's I went to Snockered to bolster my resolve with a few strong drinks. For about an hour I played pool with him for money. I ended up winning all his money and, when I left, he was waiting for me in the bushes. I gave him a hundred dollars and told him to stay out of trouble. I didn't see him anymore. I went from there to Raylene's, leaving for home around ten. The next morning Chief Wainwright showed up with a search warrant. This Henderson guy said he found a gun in my car. It wasn't mine. Someone must be framing me. Jellico said he'd handle everything and for me not to worry."

"Bill, you're charged with murder. If the jury finds you guilty they'll strap you into that chair they've got at the Tucker Farm and send twenty thousand volts through your body. I've heard of people's heads blowing off."

"What do you want me to do? Jellico said he'd handle everything. He said anything I did would be to my detriment."

Their meal came but neither felt like eating. Bill took his fork and shoved around a few pinto beans, never actually bringing one to his mouth. Faye buttered her bread and looked at Bill. Could he be the one? He didn't kill Raylene. Probably didn't kill Galen either. She knew that if she and Bill ever had a relationship she would have to be positive that he was completely innocent. Someone needed to find the real killer and then she'd entertain the idea of dating Bill.

"I think you ought to have Mr. Jellico inform you of how he's planning on saving your bacon. You two should have strategy sessions on a regular basis. And I'd like to participate. I've read lots of murder mysteries."

"I'll see what Jellico says."

CHAPTER 11—THE CITY COUNCIL

"I thought we voted not to have those public restrooms." Harold Greenleaf looked around the room seeking a consensus.

Mayor Bob stood up. "Gentlemen, the anonymous donor asked if he could construct the public restrooms on city property. He offered to do it at his own expense and we voted against it. So these new facilities were built on private property. I understand there's been a fund set up for regular maintenance. The architects have supplied me with drawings of what they'll look like." He opened a worn briefcase, took out some rolled up paper, removed the rubber band, and passed around the separated sheets.

"My God, this looks better than what I've got at home. And they've got showers and lockers. Will the maintenance cover the landscaping as well?" Paul Nelson was starting to reconsider his earlier negative position.

"Yes. It's a turnkey operation; no expense at all to the city." Mayor Bob closed his briefcase and sat down. "I think what we need to consider today is the new park being built at Ridley's farm. Our anonymous donor has bought the portion that butts up to Main Street and is in the process of paying for having dirt pushed around. I saw where yesterday several trucks brought loads of massive rocks. Bulldozers are now moving them into place. The architect, who designed the park, has been on the site every day of its construction. He says the boulders are just there for aesthetics. There's going to be winding walkways, a playground area, and a bathhouse. There's also a group of workers building out the spring so that the citizens of Dancing Deer can swim in it year-round. When it's finished, the park will be deeded to the city. My wife can't wait. She's already looking at bathing suits."

Harold Greenleaf raised his hand. "Is there anything that says we can't sell the park after it's ours and use the money to lower property taxes? I could care less about a swimming hole. I'm damn upset about how much money I'm forking over to subsidize the schools when I don't even have a kid in school."

Mayor Bob shook his head. "Nothing's been written down yet. I guess it would depend on how the contract's worded."

Paul Nelson stood up. "Gentlemen, has anyone heard about the donor providing a Little League Baseball Park?"

"Damnit. That's the last straw. Five years from now and I won't even know our town. It'll be too uppity for me to live in. Is he also going to put in a public golf course?"

Jerry Millhouse raised his hand for the first time. "Who would we talk to if we wanted to approve the golf course?"

"Damnit Jerry, I was only wisecracking."

"Okay. About the Little League ballpark. Anyone know anything? No? My boy offered to help build it, but I told him to stow it. Now I'm feeling a little ashamed and promised I'd find out."

"On the way over I saw construction workers installing park benches on the sidewalks. You know all those offsets that looked like short passing lanes. Actually, each is going to have a trash receptacle and a park-bench."

"Well if you want my opinion, I think someone like *Life* magazine is subsidizing the work and plans on exploiting our small-town American lifestyle. I won't have it."

"Are we voting on anything today?"

"No."

"Well let's adjourn, so we can go to old man Ridley's farm and put in our two-cents worth."

CHAPTER 12—THE PARTNERSHIP

Jellico looked through the box of evidence delivered from the prosecutor's office. He had formally requested what the state had through the discovery process. In the box everything was marked with an identification number and individually packaged. There was the gun found in Bill's car, Raylene's purse and its contents, pictures of Raylene and her apartment, and pictures of Hamelin and the area where he was found. There were copies of the autopsy reports, statements from several witnesses, the .45 slug found on the street, and a list of fingerprints and the people they were matched with. A lot of evidence. Most of it pointing at Bill. A soft knock on his office door.

"Just a minute." Jellico put the lid on the box and ambled toward the door. An attractive blond held out her hand.

"Mr. Jellico, I'm Harriet Potter—Willie's wife. May I talk with you?"

"Yes, I do believe we have some common ground."

Harriet sat in a big comfortable chair next to the box of evidence. "Have you formulated a plan?"

"No, ma'am. The state can prove Bill had a gun that was recently discharged, that he was at the scene of the crime, that he had a confrontation with Mr. Hamelin, and that he and Miss Carlisle had just broken their ten-year sexual relationship. They think Mr. Hamelin robbed Bill and are trying to get evidence that Miss Carlisle was blackmailing him to keep their encounters secret."

"Willie didn't do it, Mr. Jellico. You've got to punch holes in their case." Harriet took out a small notebook and pen. "Is there anything I can do to help? I understand witnesses sometimes withhold observations from people they find intimidating. I might be able to elicit information you would have a hard time getting."

Jellico took off the lid to the box. "Mrs. Potter, you might be right. How about I give you a couple of the witnesses to talk to and you can help me determine how effective they will be on the stand. And where their testimony might be vulnerable."

He handed her Bear Radisson's statement. "This might be a good place to start." Harriet read over the statement while Jellico fumbled through the box for other statements. He held out the two from Katy and Faye. "Mrs. Potter, have you ever seen anyone work a crime scene?"

"No. But I'd like to."

"Okay. Meet me at Raylene's apartment building this evening around six. If we can find the slug that killed Mr. Hamelin we can put a big dent in the state's case. That is, if it came from a different gun than Bill's."

"I'll be there. May I take these statements? They're on onion-skin paper—probably copies."

Harriet went looking for Pepe. Poor Willie, she thought. How does he get himself into all these scrapes?

Pepe was reading a book he had unpacked. Things were pretty boring. No one to talk to, no newspapers he could read, no women showing an interest.

"Pepe, do you have a minute?"

"For you, I have all day."

"Pepe, we've got to find the murderer of Raylene and Mr. Hamelin. If we don't they're gonna fry Willie. I'm supposed to meet his lawyer at the murder scene this evening. Come with me. Your sharp intellect might be just what we need. What do you say?"

"Sounds like an adventure to me. How did you convince him to let you participate?"

"I don't think he has a detective to help him track down leads. I offered to do it to help Willie and he agreed. Let's eat and head that way. It's about fifteen blocks. Not so far a walk for someone as fit as you."

"Harriet, you are such a manipulator."

74

CHAPTER 13—THE CRIME SCENE

"Mr. Jellico . . . " Harriet walked briskly to Bill's lawyer. "Mr. Jellico, let me introduce you to Pepe Martel."

Pepe was a few steps behind Harriet. She was always in such a hurry. He had fallen back when they first left the Ritz Hotel Bistro and he walked the entire fifteen blocks feeling like he was being towed. He reached the two and held out his hand.

"Mr. Jellico, Pepe was in the French Foreign Legion for a number of years. When he left he became a consultant to the Paris Police Department. He's now here in Dancing Deer doing research on an international murder mystery. In addition to his practical experience, he's written books about criminal and deviant behavior. I've told him we could use his astute observations. However, he doesn't speak English so I'll have to be his interpreter." Jellico shook hands with Pepe and asked Harriet what was his nationality.

"Why, French, of course."

"Then he couldn't have been in the French Foreign Legion as they are men from other countries serving the French government."

"I'll ask." Harriet turned to Pepe. "Is there a military organization in France dedicated to high intrigue? Quick."

Pepe wondered what she was talking about. "How about the French Resistance?"

Harriet turned back to Jellico. "He says he's Belgian."

Pepe walked over to the evergreen bushes planted in front of the apartment building.

"I dunno, Mrs. Potter. What good would he be? I mean, he's in a foreign country, he won't understand our legal system, he doesn't speak English, he won't be able to understand what any of the witnesses say . . . ."

Pepe tapped Harriet on her shoulder. He held a piece of broken glass. "Tell Mr. Jellico someone fired a shot from inside that center apartment on the third floor." One corner of the glass was missing part of a small circle.

Jellico looked at the glass fragment and the bits of glass glazing still attached. He then looked up at the window frame on the third floor covered with cardboard. "This is wonderful. Ask him where the slug that killed Hamelin might be?"

Pepe looked at the picture of Hamelin's body and the tape outlining his body on the sidewalk. He practiced a few falls to determine how close he might be to simulating what happened to the body when it was shot so that it ended up as it did. In a few minutes he shrugged his shoulders and Bill's new defense team entered the building.

Pepe said, "Harriet, mention to Mr. Jellico that nothing should be moved until we've seen the entire apartment. We need to visualize what happened. Re-enact, so to speak, in our minds, the sequence of events. If we rearrange things we corrupt the scene."

"Jellico, don't touch anything. Pepe's going to tune his inner forces to re-create what happened. He'll know momentarily who the culprit is."

"He can do that?"

"Until he knows for sure he won't tell us anything, but he'll have a good idea once he gets a handle on all the clues. It's a game to him. Who's the smartest—the crook or the detective? He's the best."

The three investigators walked through the entrance hall to the staircase and ascended to the second floor. Pepe noticed a bank of mailboxes in the entranceway with the names of tenants and the apartment number for each. Besides the front door, there was a back door at the end of a corridor of apartment doors. On the second floor, Harriet and Jellico were already in the room when Pepe made the last stair step. Miss Carlisle's apartment was at the end of the corridor next to another back door. A locked back door. There were black smudges everywhere fingerprints might be found: on the stair rail, Miss Carlisle's door knob, the door edges, and the peephole. Inside, everything was a tumbled mess.

"We haven't touched a thing. The police took pictures before anything was moved. After they scoured the area for evidence, they returned everything back to agree with the pictures." Harriet had a tablet of paper and a pen. "I'll take your notes. Have you found anything yet?"

"You might ask Mr. Jellico if there are any fingerprints yet to be matched. I'm especially interested in the thumb print on the door's peephole."

"Oh, Pepe. You really are good." Harriet affectionately squeezed Pepe's arm then turned to Jellico. "Pepe thinks the murderer left his thumbprint on the observation hole in her door. Have they matched it up with anyone yet?"

Pepe was at the desk. He recognized it. He slid the center desk drawer out, back in, then out again. Then he got down on his knees and reached up from under the desk to the area behind the center drawer. With a click the drawer pulled out another six inches, revealing a hidden compartment. Pepe bumped into Jellico when he stood up.

"My God, it's her address book. And two savings registers. Mr. Martel, you are astounding." Jellico was flipping through the book.

"I told you, he's the best."

Pepe was down on the floor crawling around with his head just inches above the area rug. In a few minutes he moved to the bathroom. He went through her medicine cabinet, make-up drawer, and linen closet. In the kitchen he opened her icebox, pantry, and trash container.

"Harriet, have you got any pictures showing the trash container?"

"I think there are several of the kitchen. The trash should be in one of them."

"Harriet, Raylene didn't use any real names. Not unless someone's named Sweet Cheeks, Pookie, Sugar Bear, or Daddy Longlegs. And it's not really an address book. More like a calendar. Look how many entries there are on Thursdays."

Jellico sat down on the edge of the bed. Back in the kitchen, Pepe looked through her cabinets. In the one behind the door to her pantry he found several stacked boxes of men's toiletries. It looked like each client had different tastes for his shaving cream, toothpaste, shampoo, and aftershave. Each box also contained a razor, toothbrush, and comb. Raylene might be a prostitute but she was one who practiced her profession with skill and thought.

"Jellico, I think when Pepe's through it's time for us to go somewhere for a strategy session."

CHAPTER 14—THE EVICTION

The truck driver rolled down his window and, leaning a fat face out, yelled, "Hey, you. You want to make some money?"

"Sure. I got to kill anybody?" Evan was sitting on a bench beside a brand new public rest room. He'd read about someone building three of them free of charge for the city and the city wanted them torn down.

"Maybe the bank manager. His boss might be putting out a contract on him as we speak." The truck driver got out of his truck and walked over to Evan. "I have to load everything from the Ghent building and haul it back to Skunk Hollow. They been kicked out of their temporary quarters and ain't been able to find another location. If you'll help load it up I'll pay you for your time."

"How much?" Evan folded the paper and laid it on the bench.

"How's about five dollars here and another five to help me unload it in Skunk Hollow?"

"How much stuff we talking about?"

"Hell, man, you got something else to do? It's just a one-room office and a lobby with a couple more desks. Not much but damn hard to handle by one man. Tell you what. I'll pay you ten dollars here and I'll find someone else back home."

"Let's do it."

Evan got in the truck. They drove two blocks to the Ghent Building and parked in the back. It was a brick two-story on Main Street. There were two windows on the first floor in the front and no others on any side on any floor. Behind the building was a small employee parking lot off an alleyway. The truck driver pulled into one of the empty parking spaces and backed to a heavy metal door.

"Come on. If we work hard we can get it all loaded in a couple of hours." The truck driver held out his hand. "I'm Reuben. You got a name?"

"Yeah. Evan."

After shaking, Reuben took a large ring of keys from the glove box. He was painfully slow, his massive arms ending with arthritically gnarled hands. He had a problem gripping the key and inserting it into the lock.

"Mister, let me help you with that?"

Reuben handed Evan the key ring. "Thanks, I been having trouble lately. Can't even brush my teeth anymore. Need a toothbrush with a handle like a baseball bat."

Evan shoved the key into the lock and turned it. He heard a definite thunk as the deadbolt slid out of its receiver. He pulled on the door. It was heavy and only swung wide when Evan pulled with both hands on the handle and pushed with one foot on the door casing. Both men peeked inside. Without windows and the only light coming through the doorway from an overcast day, it was dark and ominous. Reuben took the keys back to the truck.

Over his shoulder, he said, "I'll get a flashlight."

With the flashlight sending out a scant ray, they hunted for a light switch.

"They weren't supposed to turn off the utilities." Reuben found the switch and, when flipped, a single bulb dimly lit the room. He said, "These people were awful miserly. No windows, pitiful lighting—no wonder they went out of business. Must've been paranoid too. Damn heavy door, thick walls. Listen. You can't hear a damn thing in here."

"What kind of business were they in?"

"Money. For years they were the only bank around and then the First Bank and Trust of Dancing Deer opened up. With a snazzy building, cheerful tellers, and a liberal lending policy to compete against, the Ghent's went broke. Then for several years Potter's bank was the only one of consequence until some new investors shoveled large stacks of money into the coffers of a small bank in Skunk Hollow. Then the management of that bank thought, with Bill Potter's trial and their extra money, they were given a golden opportunity to expand. However, they hadn't considered the savvy of Mr. Potter. He's just like his old man. Ain't nobody gonna get the best of him. Now those boys back in Skunk Hollow are in full retreat. I've heard they're worried Potter's planning to expand their way."

Reuben and Evan were now walking toward the front of the building. With two windows letting in a small amount of light the rooms up front were dimly lit on their own. Reuben turned on lights as he found them.

"All right, let's start with these desks. We'll take the chairs next and set them upside down on the desks. That'll leave the filing cabinets and boxes. I got a dolly if we need it."

For the rest of the morning Evan helped Reuben load up the failed Skunk Hollow expansion bank. The employees had already boxed the small items and files from the filing cabinets. When it was time to load the boxes, Evan had a chance to look at the lock on the heavy back door. From inside, the deadbolt extended or retreated with the twist of a knob.

"Where's the safe?"

"Don't know. Maybe we better look. In fact, we better check all the rooms in case some wise-ass wanted his desk separated from the others."

Safety deposit boxes and a stack of teller tills were in a walk-in safe adjacent to the office they had just moved. The walls, floor, and ceiling were covered with slabs of sheet steel. The thick safe door stood open, showing a wide rubber gasket that made the safe airtight when the door closed. Nothing to be moved was inside. There was one more empty office on the first floor and a restroom. On the second floor was another restroom and four small window-less offices. There was also one large open room that, with the discoloration on the floor, looked like it once had held filing cabinets. When the last of the boxes were loaded, Reuben reached into his pocket and paid Evan ten dollars. They shook hands.

Evan said, "Thanks." He stuffed the money into his pocket and walked off. Evan turned and ran into the building when Reuben went to retrieve the keys. When Reuben returned he looked around for his helper.

"Evan?" Now where could he have gone? Left me here to lockup the damn place. Reuben peered into the dark building. He slammed the door shut and, shaking his head, fumbled with the keys.

Evan silently waited while Reuben, with his arthritic hands, worked on getting the key to lock the door.

CHAPTER 15—THE EVIDENCE

Jellico handed Pepe the box of evidence from the DA's office. The first thing Pepe pulled out was the gun. It was a short-barreled .38 revolver. Pepe opened the cylinder and gave it a twirl. He used his thumb to pull back the hammer and then eased it back into place. He set it down and picked up Raylene's bank register. Regular deposits of three hundred dollars per week. Only two large checks per month. He held out the register to Harriet, pointing to the monthly checks.

"Pepe, honey, this one's for her mother. She suffers from dementia and lives in a private hospital. This other one moves money to her savings account."

Pepe thought to himself, I must be making headway. From "honey" it's not all that far to "I think I'll slip into something more comfortable." Pepe pointed to two other entries occurring regularly.

"Bus fares. She visits her mother on weekends." Pepe considered. Bus fares, two or three times a month. Two different amounts. Must be two different locations. Pepe then picked up the address book. No addresses, four telephone numbers—each entered at six p.m. on Mondays, Tuesdays, Wednesdays, and Fridays beside a pet name she'd given each of her four regular clients. There were other entries like doctor's appointments and cleaners on each day until the telephone number and nothing entered after for the rest of the night. Thursdays were different. She had entered initials for each hour starting at two p.m., with some entries on the half-hour, all the way until midnight.

"That telephone number for Friday is Willie's."

"What about these others?" Pepe pointed to the other numbers.

"Jellico asked if I would call to see who might answer."

Jellico was in an adjacent chair trying to understand the conversation. Pepe handed Harriet the telephone. She dialed the number for Monday. After a couple of rings a woman answered the phone and said "Manhattan Club."

"Is there a Mr. Smith there?"

"No Mr. Smith tonight."

Harriet hung up the telephone and asked Jellico if he knew anything about the Manhattan Club.

"It's a gentleman's club above a small café downtown. They have poker games most week nights. Only the town's best citizens are allowed to play. Why didn't you ask for Sugar Bear?"

Harriet shook her head then dialed Tuesday's number. An operator said that line had been disconnected. When she dialed Wednesday's number she heard a familiar voice but couldn't place it.

"I think I might have a wrong number. Is there a Dorothy there?"

"No. There's no Dorothy here. Maybe you dialed the wrong number. What number were you calling?"

"Chief Wainwright, is that you?"

"Yeah. Who are you?"

"This is Harriet Potter. I must've written your number down without putting a name with it. I'm sorry to bother you."

"Mrs. Potter, I don't give out my home telephone number. How did you come by it?"

"Sorry, Chief. I don't know. I just have a telephone number but no name. I was going to throw it away but decided to call first. Good night, sir." She hung up the telephone before Chief Wainwright had an opportunity to say anything else.

"My, my. Our chief of police goes by 'Pookie.'" Jellico folded his arms over a massive stomach. "It looks like she had a number to reach each client in case something came up or if they didn't show. Pretty influential clientele, I might add. She must charge a hundred dollars per month, with Bill paying her rent. But what do you think about Thursdays? She's got a dozen entries for that one day and night. Must have been for quickies—spending cash."

Harriet relayed all this information to Pepe and then, getting up from her chair, looked through her room's window at the few night lights in downtown Dancing Deer. "Sweet Cheeks." Willie is Raylene's

"Sweet Cheeks." He's been seeing a prostitute every Friday night for ten years. And I wanted to make up. How can a sane woman forgive a man who pays for sex. I must be crazy.

She returned to Pepe, who asked, "Where might someone buy a gun in Dancing Deer?" Harriet asked Jellico, who told her Eberly's Sporting Goods was the only place he knew of.

Pepe stood up. "I'm going to the bar for a few drinks before I retire for the evening. Would you care to join me? I think I have tomorrow planned."

Jellico put the evidence back in the box then picked it up. "This has been a productive day. I'm glad to have both of you working with me on this." He walked to the door. "I'll talk to you tomorrow."

Downstairs Pepe ordered a glass of Armagnac. Harriet ordered a gin martini. When the drinks came Pepe held his up and said, "Here's to love. It's like quicksilver. You can hold it forever in the palm of your hand but try to clutch it and it darts away."

"Pepe, you are so smart. I wish I had your grasp of things. I feel like I'm trying to find something that's just out of reach or around the corner. My whole life I've been looking for it. Somehow I think it's here."

During the next hour Harriet drank six more martinis and when she started slipping from the bar stool Pepe steadied her, then suggested he help her to her room.

"You wouldn't take advantage of an inebriated woman would you?"

"No."

"Too bad."

Harriet fumbled with the key, then handed it to Pepe, who opened the door. He helped her inside and left when she went into the bathroom.

CHAPTER 16—MARY

"Eston, you've been such a good boy, I think we ought to stop at Eudy's Drug and Fountain and get you a stick of licorice and me a strawberry soda." Eston gave his mother a questioning look. He didn't like licorice. "Okay, I'll eat the licorice and we'll share the soda."

For the last few months she'd been having the strangest requests. Her body was telling her it wanted foods not normally supplied. How long had it been since she'd tasted licorice? "The doctor said they're due in two more weeks. You're going to have someone to play with Eston. Not at first, of course, but soon."

"Vroom, vroom." The little boy rolled a toy along the seat, trying to keep the wheels astraddle the stitching.

Mary had taken her husband to work so she would have the car. Now that the time was drawing near, her doctor wanted to see her every week. He said everything's coming along nicely. She wondered what he'd been drinking. Her ankles were swelling, she couldn't sleep, she couldn't stay away from the bathroom long enough to get anything done, her back hurt. She thought men should have to take their turn. Pulling into the driveway, she was glad to be home.

So this is where that son-of-a-bitch lives. Looks smaller in the daylight. Driving up in that big black Packard like he owned the place. I'd recognize him anywhere . . . and that car. Took a two-by-four to us. Left us lying helpless in the parking lot. I'll kill him. We agreed if we ever found him we'd make him regret ever coming to Wind Springs. Now Terrell's dead and Gleason's in prison. I'll have to do it myself. Why the hell did they have to go and rob that laundry? Everyone knew that foreigner kept a gun handy. Shot Terrell in the back. I ought to kill him too.

Evan Bonds parked his car down the street and walked to Bill's house. He had a gun in his pocket and planned on getting revenge for an episode three months earlier when Bill Potter and Jed Calhoun stopped on their way to find Bill's daughter in Springfield. Bill and the Bonds boys had an argument over the only parking spot at the City Café. Bill manhandled the three of them with a piece of lumber and left town as fast as he could. There wasn't a day gone by that Evan and Gleason didn't think about it.

Evan pulled his gun and knocked on the door. He'd followed Potter from that apartment. Evan knew where Potter lived . . . and where Potter would die.

"Hell, he's not home."

Evan walked around to the back, broke a bedroom window, and crawled inside. It didn't look like a house Potter would live in. Kid's toys, something slow-cooking on the stove, dishes drying on a towel. Probably has a wife. Evan heard a car drive up, looked around for a place to hide, and stepped behind a floor-length curtain.

"Eston, get your marbles. Remember what I told you. Don't bet more than you can afford to lose. Only bet the dates and keep the taws to shoot with."

Mary had been working with Eston and he was fast becoming a force in the neighborhood. He now had a sizable sack of marbles he'd won and had dreams of completely wiping out his major competition. Eston grabbed his sack and ran looking for a game.

Evan was thinking he'd gotten into the wrong house. He could see the back end of the car. It was a decrepit old Ford. Time to go. He adjusted his stocking mask, lurched from his hiding place, and ran toward the front door, shoving the woman into the fireplace as he sailed past. Mary landed on her back with her hand falling on the fireplace poker. She rolled to her knees, pulled herself up with the help of the fireplace mantle, and prepared to do battle with the intruder.

Evan stepped on a toy fire truck, slid, and tumbled backwards with his feet slung above his head. He looked up just in time to see something shiny come crashing toward his face. He jerked to the side and the weapon slammed into the soft tissue between his neck and shoulder. He yelled out in pain, scrambled to his feet, and ran for the door. Another swat made contact with his thigh. He fell into the hall tree, getting a hat hook caught in the mouth opening to his mask. With the mask now pulled sideways he couldn't see. He crawled to the door as another blow landed on his back. Hell, this was just like the parking lot. The door wouldn't open. Another blow to the back.

"Aaaccckkk. My water broke." Mary stumbled to a chair, holding her stomach, holding her twins.

The front door popped open and the hall tree fell, hitting Evan on his backside propelling him through the front door and into the yard. Evan staggered to his feet and limped as fast as he could to his car.

CHAPTER 17—THE QUESTIONS

Pepe sauntered into the Ritz Hotel Bistro for breakfast. Harriet would be down in a few minutes. They'd eat, then take a taxi to talk to the witnesses. He ordered, ate, and read his book. Where was that woman? Where was his waitress? Pepe asked the replacement waitress for a telephone. After being in the states for three months he'd picked up a few English words. He couldn't carry on a conversation but the words for coffee, several alcoholic beverages, telephone, toilet, cigarettes, car, and a few others mysteriously appeared when needed.

"House or outside line?"

He knew she'd asked a question by the rise in pitch she gave at the end of her sentence. What she'd asked, Pepe didn't know, so he did the customary shoulder shrug and tilt of his head. The waitress plugged the telephone cord into an outlet on the wall next to his table and handed Pepe the phone. He'd get the hang of this yet. He dialed her room. It rang eight times before a sleepy voice answered.

"Harriet, I'm off to talk to that guy at the pool hall. I'll let you know what he says at lunch."

"You will not. I'll be downstairs in fifteen minutes."

"I'm finished eating. How about I come up to your room and wait while you get ready. We can talk through the wall."

"Okay. I'll slip into the shower. The door will be unlocked."

Pepe thought maybe he'd slip into the shower with her. It wouldn't be the first time he'd showered twice in the same morning. He whistled as he walked to the elevator. Before the door closed, Bill Potter came aboard and pushed the third floor elevator button. He smiled at Pepe, put both hands in his pockets, and then took one out to adjust his ribbon tie. At the third floor he stood back to let Pepe out. After all, it was only proper. The little Frenchman had to be twenty years Bill's senior.

Pepe walked down the hall to Harriet's room, opened the door, and walked in. When he turned to shut it he found Bill standing in the doorway with a perplexed look on his face. He paused and stood aside to allow Bill to enter. Without speaking both went to the seating area and sat in opposite chairs.

From the shower Harriet said, "Did you bring coffee, Pepe?"

"No, love. I've had so much coffee waiting on you I didn't even think of it. I'll order some from room service."

Harriet opened the bathroom door and walked into the room wrapped in a towel and with another wound around her hair. "That's okay. I'll do . . . hello, Willie. We having a party?"

"We might, but I'm not sure I'm invited."

"Have you met Pepe Martel? He's helping me clear your good name. Willie, do you know anyone named Sweet Cheeks?"

"Uh . . . not a common name. But I do recall hearing it somewhere."

"Let me see. How does this sound? Bill 'Sweet Cheeks' Potter? Has a kind of ring don't you think?"

"My God. You've found Raylene's address book."

"If we found anything it was because of Pepe's uncanny ability to piece together small fragments of information. I'm not sure what Jellico wants you to know so, if you don't mind, instead of us answering your questions, maybe you'll answer ours?"

"Sure. Whatever you want."

Harriet sat down on a loveseat. "Pepe, what questions do you have for Willie?"

"Ask him if we can borrow his car."

"What else?"

"What does he drink when he visits Raylene? Does he like beer?" Harriet wrote down the questions in her notebook and looked at Pepe for more. "Ask him if he ever visited Faye Spencer on the third floor. If he has a key to Raylene's apartment and, if he does, did Raylene know about it? How about the back door? Where'd he park his car on Friday nights? On the night of the murder? Does he know who the other clients are? Does he know how many there were? Does he . . ."

"Slow down, Pepe."

92

"Okay. Does he know why she had two savings accounts with only one getting regular deposits? What did she normally do on weekends? What was her reaction to him terminating their relationship? What was she wearing when he came by Friday evening? How long did he stay? Did she always keep her door locked? Did she own a gun? Why would someone want to frame him? Does he have any enemies?"

"Just a second, Pepe. I've got a cramp in my hand." Harriet laid down her pen and shook her hand. "Okay. What else?"

"Did anyone see or hear him talk to Hamelin when he gave the hundred dollars? Does he always wear cowboy boots and jeans?"

"Hold on." Harriet laid her notebook down and used the telephone to order breakfast, a thermos of coffee, cream, and three coffee cups. "Continue."

"Hell, I've now forgotten what I've already asked."

"In that case, I'll get ready while you two find common ground." Harriet walked into her bathroom.

When the food came Pepe reached into his pocket but Bill made a hand gesture to the hotel employee, who hurried out of the room after wheeling the cart close to their chairs. Bill poured two cups of coffee and handed one to Pepe. They drank in silence. In a few minutes Harriet emerged with her hair arranged and make-up applied. Dressed in black, she was bra-less in a sweater, a free flowing skirt, and boots. Both men watched her bounce into the room. Pepe liked the way she looked and let her know by a low whistle. Bill uncrossed his leg and then crossed the other.

Harriet took her breakfast to the loveseat. "Willie, tell me what a regular Friday night was like?" She smeared a large chunk of sweet butter over a piece of toasted raison bread.

"I'd arrive pretty close to six. I was told not to be early but I could be as late as I wanted. I always came in the back door. Since I was the one who rented the apartment I had keys to the front and the second-floor back door—which was always kept locked—and her apartment. Someone on the ground floor usually locked the front door around midnight. I never used my key to her door. I always knocked.

"She'd have the lights dimmed, soft music playing on the radio, and candles lighting the table. I'd sit in a comfortable chair positioned so I could see her work in the kitchen. She'd bring me a glass of wine and feed me small tidbits of food by hand. Sometimes she'd sit on my lap and run her fingers through my hair. I could feel the tension of the day ebb from my body as I wallowed in the smells and warmth of a woman totally devoted to making me happy. When I was aroused enough to whisk her off to the bedroom, she'd slowly walk in a suggestive way to the kitchen to finish preparing our meal.

"We didn't eat seating across from each other but side by side, almost touching. She kept my wine and water glasses filled, sometimes wiping my lip with her napkin. We ate, taking small bites of lovingly cooked and garnished dishes she spent most of the afternoon preparing. I told her about my day. The good things made her smile and the bad things made her reach out and cover my hand with hers. When I asked her about her day she'd only tell me about the preparations she'd made for my visit. I really don't know much about her but she knows everything about me.

"After the meal we'd go into the living room and dance to Tommy Dorsey, listen to the radio, or play-act from scripts she had written. They were sometimes funny, sometimes sad, and always entertaining. Sometimes she sang love songs she had written. Around ten we'd go to bed. She was the most amazing woman I've ever known.

"The next morning I'd lie in bed and smell my breakfast being cooked with the earthy scent of freshly brewed coffee seeping down the hallway, seeking me out. In the bathroom she'd have my toiletries arranged. I never saw any evidence of any of her other clients. I know there must have been others but she kept me unaware of their existence. I'm glad. I never wanted to think of her with another man. After breakfast I had to leave. The minute I was out the door I started thinking about the next Friday evening."

"Willie, I think I love her myself."

CHAPTER 18—REPORT

"Honey, how do you feel?" Charles Jimmerson stood at the doorway to his wife's hospital room wringing his hands.

"A little groggy. Have you seen them? Are they okay? Do you know when they'll be bringing them to me?"

"They're beautiful. A boy and a girl. The doctor said they're fraternal twins. We have to choose names."

"I want to call the girl Elizabeth. You can name the boy."

"Tell me about the burglar. There's a policeman outside wanting to talk with you when you feel like it."

"There's not much to tell. When Eston and I got home from the doctor's office, he was already in the house. Before I had much more than taken off my coat, he come busting out from behind the dining-room drapes and pushed me on the way to the door. He fell on a toy and I hit him with the fireplace poker. He made it out the door and my water broke. That's it."

"Did he steal anything?"

"I don't think so. We haven't got anything worth stealing anyway."

"I'm going to tell Jellico. This might have something to do with Mr. Potter's case."

"Charles, how are things at the bank? You're putting in so many hours now that Mr. Potter has made you in charge. You're always so tired when you get home I don't want to trouble you."

"We've lost a few customers. The first day after Bill's . . . Mr. Potter's charge came out in the newspaper we had a long line of people wanting their money. We were ready and when it appeared the bank could handle all requests the clamoring died down. Then the bank from Skunk Hollow opened a branch office across the street and had people walk up and down the sidewalks carrying signs telling the good citizens of Dancing Deer they'd better get their money out of our bank while they still could.

"Mr. Potter went to their expansion bank and stood in line like everyone else. People were wondering what he was doing there. When his turn came he said he wanted to close his account. They called the home office to determine how much he had on deposit. It was twenty thousand dollars and they couldn't honor it. He got mad at them for advertising that keeping money in his bank was risky when checks for valid deposits in their bank wouldn't be honored.

He's plenty smart. After that the people in lines at both banks fizzled. He finally had to threaten the Skunk Hollow people with bank fraud before they wired the money. He used those funds to help purchase the building they were in and made them move out. When they tried to relocate no one would rent them any space. I think most of the property owners have outstanding loans and didn't want Bill calling in their notes.

"Right now our biggest problem is the bank examiners. They're trying to determine if Bill co-mingled the bank's money with his own. It's just one problem after another. I feel like I'm on a fast train to Detroit."

"Darling, I know Bill Potter is one smart man because he's turned everything over to you and you can handle anything."

CHAPTER 19—THE STATEMENTS

The rain started sometime during the night and continued off and on all morning. When Bill gave the Packard's keys to Harriet he had reservations. Cars were hard to come by. The automobile manufacturers had changed over, even before the United States entered the war. Instead of automobiles they started producing tanks, jeeps, amphibious landing craft, troop transport trucks, and airplanes.

Rubber was hard to come by. Most cars now sported bald tires and the repair services made a killing keeping the older vehicles on the road. It wasn't uncommon for a person using all his gas rations also to have a couple of flats per week.

"Harriet, you might let Mr. Martel drive. The streets are slippery with the rain and I'd feel better if someone with a little experience was behind the wheel."

"Really, Willie. You never were able to keep me under your thumb. You think I'm going to let you now? Pepe needs to think. If I'm able to get you acquitted it'll be because Pepe comes up with the information Jellico needs. I'm going to give him all the help I can and right now that means chauffeuring him around in your car.

"I want to talk with you this evening. Willie, let's have a drink in the bar when I get back."

"Okay, but be careful."

"I'll call when I get back. We got to get Pepe's questions answered."

On the way to Snockered Harriet told Pepe about Bill's relationship with Raylene, then gave him a translation of Bear Radisson's statement. Pepe thought the prosecution was going to use Bill's confrontation with Hamelin and probable robbery as his motivation for killing the man. He also thought their premise wasn't with merit. Bill was too wealthy to kill somebody for such a pittance. However, if Hamelin gave any problem to Raylene then Bill would do whatever he thought necessary to keep her safe or retaliate in the worst way if he thought Hamelin had hurt her. They came away with little new knowledge. Bill had several strong drinks but wasn't so drunk that it affected his vision or slurred his speech. Several people had witnessed his steady hand with the pool cue. Bear said Bill told him something weighed heavy on his mind. Also, one of the sheriff's deputies questioned Hamelin after Bill drove off.

Their next stop was back at the murder scene, but this time to the third floor where Katy waited. They had an appointment. When they arrived, Katy produced a tray of Earl Grey tea and scones from the bakery two blocks away. Pepe sat down with his biscuit and tea to watch Katy's reaction to Harriet's questions.

"Mrs. Hamelin . . ."

"Please, call me Katy."

"Very well. Katy, in your statement you said you were unaware your husband was outside and that Faye was working late, not arriving 'till midnight."

"Yes. That's correct."

"And when Faye arrived you were still awake reading a novel. That Faye made no mention of anyone loitering around and neither of you heard any arguments or gunshots at any time during the night. That the police sirens were the first indication you had that anything was happening."

"Yes."

"So why are you listed as a witness for the prosecution? It doesn't appear you have any evidence to support the state's case."

"I don't know. Maybe they want me to testify about Galen's volatile temper. He'd fly off the handle with only the least bit of provocation. He once broke a man's jaw for talking to me at a party. He was insanely jealous and jumpy. He thought the Canneli brothers were out to kill him. He owed them a lot of money."

"I see. So if Willie won money from him playing pool, then he would try and get it back somehow."

"Yes, leaving Mr. Potter bleeding in the bushes."

"And it's possible that the Canneli brothers found him here and they were the ones who killed him."

"No. There's no way they could know he was here."

"Have you told this to the police?"

"Only to Sheriff Shodtoe." Katy picked up the tray of sweets and walked over to Pepe, who sat on the couch. She placed one on his napkin then refilled his tea cup and sat down beside him. Looking at Harriet she said, "Mr. Jellico says he's a famous private detective from Belgium. Will you ask if he knows Hercule Poirot?"

Harriet turned to Pepe. "She wants to know how old you are. You remind her of her father."

"Tell her I'm as old as dirt."

"Pepe, you are so . . . how can I say this . . . so . . . so virile. Are there any questions you want me to ask her?"

"Ask her about the gunshot through the window."

"Katy, Pepe said that he once showed Monsieur Poirot how to pick a lock but that, soon after, Poirot left Belgium for England and he's not seen or heard from Poirot since. Monsieur Martel also wants to know if you might need a job. His daughter is in need of a cook."

"I don't cook."

"Do you own a gun? There's been a shot through your window recently. We thought you might be trying to hit your husband while he stood outside trying to talk you into giving him a second chance."

"Yes, I have a gun, but the shot was an accident. I was only examining the weapon when it went off. The bullet almost hit a police officer in his car. I'll get it for you."

"While you do that, may I use your bathroom?"

When Harriet returned Katy was sitting on Pepe's knee. The cartridge clip had been removed from the gun and lay beside the tray of sweets. Pepe had his arms around Katy with his hands holding Katy's hands, which were holding the gun. Harriet stood in amazement in the doorway while Pepe used gestures to show Katy how to point at a target using the sight on the barrel and the one in front of the hammer. When Harriet walked into the room, Katy quickly slid off Pepe's knee, landing beside him on the couch.

Pepe sensed the tension and stood up. "I think it's time for us to go to Eberly's Sporting Goods. We told Jellico to meet us there at two."

Pepe took Katy's hand, turned it over and kissed her palm. "Enchante, Mademoiselle."

Herman Eberly looked at the .38 policeman's special. "I sell lots of these."

Pepe said, "Harriet, ask him if he special ordered those oversized grips. They wouldn't have come on a standard model."

Herman said he'd check his records and in a minute came back saying he sold the gun to Paul Nelson five years ago. The grips were ordered at the same time. Jellico said he knew Mr. Nelson and, if they wanted to go to the sheriff's office to check on the deputy's meeting with Galen, he'd head to Mr. Nelson's. They could have dinner at the bistro at six to discuss what information each party had uncovered. It was late Friday afternoon when Harriet and Pepe arrived at the sheriff's office. A weekend dispatcher said she remembered receiving the call. She retrieved her log book and was dismayed to find her entry had been erased.

"Why do you think someone erased it?"

"A lot of Sheriff Shodtoe's dealings are kept off the books. I remember him telling both deputies to find this Hamelin character and to call him the moment they did."

"Why do you think he did that? The police said they couldn't bring him in until he broke the law. They even removed the officer keeping an eye on the apartment where Mr. Hamelin's wife hid."

"I don't know. I wouldn't have told you anything but this weekend is my last. I've got a new job starting Monday, working the counter at Eudy's Drug and Fountain."

Harriet stopped writing in her notebook. "Which of the two deputies called it in?"

"Let me look on the duty roster." She left and in a few minutes returned saying it was Rafe because Ralph had scheduled duty. They worked at Snockered on their own time.

CHAPTER 20—STRATEGY SESSION

Jellico suggested the three of them invite Bill to join their group. Bill asked if Faye might participate and she brought along Katy. They had such a big party Bill decided they should step down the hall to one of the conference rooms.

Jellico said, "I'll start this off by saying the gun was purchased at Eberly's Sporting Goods five years ago. It was then stolen and used in a robbery. When the police apprehended the culprit the gun was held as evidence, kept in the property room, and never returned to its rightful owner. While in police custody it still had its serial number. Then the gun shows up in Bill's car, found by Officer Henderson, with the serial number filed off. It looks like I've got to find out more about Officer Henderson, who is responsible for the property room, and who signed the gun's custody slip if the clerk in the property room turned it over to someone."

Harriet said, "Pepe and I have found that Deputy Sheriff Rafe Johnson talked with Hamelin after Willie gave him the hundred dollars and drove to Raylene's. Also, that someone erased the entry from the dispatcher's log. In addition, the .45 slug found in the street probably was shot by Katy, at no one in particular."

Jellico stopped eating his caesar salad and said, "I think we should consider the two murders separately. The police have not found anything proving Hamelin was in Raylene's room. They have lots of unmatched fingerprints but none for Hamelin. Besides he had no reason. I think Raylene's murderer was looking for something. Her apartment was rifled. Also, someone broke into Bill's house. He probably thinks if it wasn't in Raylene's apartment, it must be in Bill's, maybe following him home after he left her apartment."

Harriet whispered to Pepe the gist of what Jellico said. Pepe then told her about the two different bus fares. "Pepe, I didn't pick up on that. You are just too much."

Jellico continued with, "And what about all those entries in Raylene's calendar for Thursday." He pulled out a sheet of paper from his valise and passed it around. "She had regular clients for Monday, Tuesday, Wednesday, and Friday but on Thursday it looks like she entertained the rest of Dancing Deer. There are initials on every hour and sometimes the half hour all the way till midnight. Does anyone have any ideas? I mean how could . . . "

Katy raised her hand. "I think those are radio shows. JB stands for Jack Benny, SK stands for The Shadow Knows, GG stands for the Great Gildersleeve, and so on. She probably took Thursdays off and listened to the radio."

"How astute, Katy. Well, that answers that."

When Harriet informed Pepe, he reached over and patted Katy's knee. When they met eye to eye Pepe gave her an appreciative wink.

Faye said, "May I have a look at Raylene's calendar?"

"No, Miss Spencer. There's too much information that's harmful to important members of our community and of no value to the defense of our case. And what's more, none of anything said here tonight can be written in your newspaper. Unless I have your word on that you must now leave."

"How about after the case has been resolved? Could I write a book about it then?"

"I have no problem with that. You should probably get written permission if you want to make any modifications to what actually happened or was said."

"Very well. I guess I agree."

"Let's get back to the gun," said Bill. "So it was probably a throw-down one of the police officers stole from the property room and planted. I don't know this Henderson. I can't see why he would want to frame me. Does anyone know anything about him?"

Katy meekly asked, "Could he be Sheriff Shodtoe's cousin? The sheriff said he had a relative on the police force."

When Harriet told Pepe what Katy said, Pepe, with his hand still on Katy's knee, gave her an affectionate squeeze. The door to the conference room opened and two waiters came in pushing a cart containing their entrees. No one said anything as their food was delivered. After the waiters left, Jellico presented Bill with a list of potential jurors.

"Bill, check these out. Use a separate sheet of paper for each. Find out if they have a bank or savings account and if they have any outstanding loans or have been turned down for a loan. Write down anything you can come up with for each."

"Bill, I might be able to help you with that. I could see if any of them have been in the news." Faye was glad to finally add something to the conversation.

Jellico finished his meal, wiped his mouth with a napkin, and said, "I have a meeting with Poo . . . with Chief Wainwright tomorrow. Harriet, what are you and Pepe going to do?"

Harriet asked Pepe, then informed Jellico, "Pepe says we're going to the bus station then to talk with Deputy Rafe Johnson and finally to Bill's old secretary, Jennifer. She's listed as a witness for the state and he wants to know why."

Bill winced, adjusted his seating position, and reached for his glass. Everyone glared at Bill as he caught the glass before it tumbled sideways to the table. "Maybe I should talk with her. When she quit she was vague as to why. I might have offended her in some way."

"And that's precisely why Harriet needs to talk with her." Jellico turned to Harriet. "I think Jennifer might be important to the state for proving motive. Be careful with the information you give out and keep good notes. I suggest you not take Pepe. Have a woman-to-woman talk. Confide to her your reservations about Bill. Tell her you think he's guilty but can't for the life of you understand why he would do it."

"Mrs. Potter, if I were to come along, we could make it a conspiracy. You know three women railing against the men who have oppressed them. And that Deputy Rafe. I can sometimes make men do the dumbest things." Katy reached under the table and pushed off Pepe's hand.

"What'd she say? Tell me what she said."

"Ssh Pepe. I'll tell you in a minute." Harriet turned to Jellico. "What do you think?"

Jellico answered, "It's your call. But if you do, you have to tell Pepe exactly what's said. I think he's our most profound thinker. The one who seems to be able to piece the puzzle together the best. The one with the best grasp on things."

CHAPTER 21—THE WITNESSES

Harriet and Katy arrived at Jennifer's house at nine in the morning. Harriet had called earlier to make sure Jennifer would be at home and if it was okay to come by. It was a little house, about a thousand square feet with a one-car detached garage linked by a white picket fence. In front of the fence bulbs were beginning to shoot green leaves through heavy pine mulch.

"Miss Gibbs, my name is Harriet Potter and this is Katy Hamelin."

"Come in, ladies. I've made cookies and herbal tea."

After removing their coats and scarves and sitting in front of the fireplace, Harriet said, "Miss Gibbs, you're listed as a witness for the prosecution. We need to know what information you might have. It's Katy's husband who was killed. We're trying to come to grips with the events as we understand them."

"Call me Jennifer. Mr. Irving told me I would probably not be called to testify. I don't know what kind of questions he'd planned on asking."

"Can you tell us why you quit working for my despicable husband?"

"Do either of you know anything about that dreadful episode on the Calhoun farm?" Harriet and Katy shook their heads. "Well, Bill sold Jed a herd of horses and made him put his farm up as collateral. The next thing I know Stanley Muldaur, the Marsden County Agricultural Extension Agent, comes into the bank with his head bandaged from just below his eyes to just above his mouth. They have a hush-hush meeting and, when Muldaur leaves, Bill gives me a deposit slip moving five thousand dollars from his personal account into Muldaur's.

"I later found out Muldaur's nose had been torn off by a wild dog and all of Jed's livestock had to be slaughtered because they had hoof and mouth disease. Jed came by to see what could be done about the loan and stomped out of Bill's office with fire in his eyes.

"After that I periodically received doctor's bills for treating Muldaur. Eventually Bill put him in a convalescent home and had me pay each year's fee in one payment from his personal account. Then one day he asked for the obituary department to a Memphis newspaper. Later that day I got a telephone call from someone at the paper giving me a list of homes for the aged each with an excessive number of health code violations. Bill had me make arrangements to transfer Muldaur from the home in Little Rock to the worst offender in Memphis. I thought he was signing the man's death warrant and I quit."

"Jennifer, I agree Bill is a scoundrel, but how does that relate to the murder of Raylene and Katy's husband?"

"I don't know. You asked why I quit. I also paid the apartment rent and utilities for Raylene. Maybe that's what he's going to ask me."

"Her telephone as well?"

"Yes, the bills are all in my desk's filing drawer. Just between the three of us, I don't know how they're going to find twelve fair people who don't already think Bill Potter is the most detestable man in Dancing Deer."

"Hello, Sherman. Do you think Harriet and I could have a word with your deputy, Rafe Johnson?"

"Katy, I was just thinking about you. Now that your husband is no longer a threat I'll have to come up with another excuse to come by and see you. Why do you want to talk to Rafe?"

"Oh, nothing, really. He's on the state's witness list and Harriet and I want to make sure Bill didn't have any accomplices. We want to see that everyone who's guilty gets punished. Why don't you take me to dinner sometime? I feel like a liberated woman."

"Betty, call Rafe and have him come to headquarters at once." Sheriff Shodtoe turned from the dispatcher back to the two ladies. "I'd like that very much. Do you have any plans for this weekend?"

"I don't think so. Let me ask Faye before I commit. You can call me tomorrow. Is there somewhere we can wait?"

"Why don't you come into my office? He's not far. I don't think he's outside the city today."

106

"I think I'll wait with Mrs. Potter until he comes and then I'll come in by myself."

Sheriff Shodtoe rubbed his hands together. Right then the roof could have fallen in and he wouldn't have noticed. The sugary way Katy was handling him, she could have told him to go straight to hell and he would have looked forward to the trip. The two ladies were escorted to a vacant office sometimes used by the state authorities when they came to do their appraisals. When Rafe arrived, the dispatcher sent him in and Katy walked down the hall to the sheriff's office.

"What can I do for you, Mrs. Potter?"

"Rafe, I'm divorcing Bill and I understand you saw him beat up Mr. Hamelin outside Snockered the night he was killed."

"Uh . . . no, I just saw them talking. It looked like your husband gave him some money and drove off. I went in to find out if he'd panhandled Bill. He was coming back out as I was going in. He said Bear told him he'd worn out his welcome. He swore Bill gave him the money and told him to stay out of trouble. I offered him a lift back into town. He wanted out in front of the newspaper's office. Said he had a friend there who would put him up for the night. I left and cruised around town before heading back to Snockered in time to see them close."

"That's too bad. I thought it might be something I could use in my divorce in case Willie beats the rap. Do you know what Mr. Irving is going to ask you on the stand?"

"Yeah. He wants me to testify that Hamelin shook Bill down for the money. But I was too far away to be able to tell. I do think that's what happened even if I can't confirm it. Sorry I can't help you, gorgeous."

"That's okay. You stick with what you know for sure." Harriet winked at Rafe and walked down the hall to the Sheriff's office. She knocked and waited a moment before entering. "Katy, we have to get back. I told that rascal husband of mine I'd have his car back by two."

When Katy reached the door she turned and blew a kiss to the sleazy sheriff. "Call me, Shermie."

Jellico couldn't wait to tell Chief Wainwright he'd located Raylene's address book. He arrived at the exact time he'd told the chief he'd be coming. "Good morning, Chief."

"What's good about it? I've got two officers sick with the flu and two funerals asking for a police escort. What do you want, Jellico?"

"I thought the funerals were tomorrow."

"They are, but these government goldbricks can take a little cold and turn it into a week's vacation. I hope I have enough officers working tomorrow to supply the two escorts. They should be buried at the same time and at the same cemetery . . . so we could use the same escort; after all, they were killed at the same time."

"Chief, I don't think you'll need an escort for Hamelin's funeral. I bet there won't be more than a handful of mourners."

"I hope you're right."

Jellico pulled out a chair and settled in. "We got any new evidence to show up since you gave me that box?"

"Maybe. You returning the first box?"

"Yeah." He reached down, picked up the box, and placed it on the table separating the two of them. "I've also found some information you might find useful." He looked at the chief to see if he had his attention. "I've found Raylene's address book, Pookie. That is what she called you?"

"Yeah. Let me see it."

"First, let's talk about it. If I give it to you it becomes part of the public domain. I don't think that would be in your best interest or in the interests of the others mentioned. First let me tell you what it contains and then if you still want it you can have it."

"Very well."

"She had regular clients on Monday, Tuesday, Wednesday, and Friday. In order, she called them Sugar Bear, Daddy Longlegs, Pookie, and Sweet Cheeks. There was a telephone number next to each pet name."

"Hence the telephone call from Harriet Potter."

"Yes. I do not believe either of her clients would consider hurting anyone they loved as dearly as they loved Raylene. Bill is so distraught he loses concentration when I talk to him. I believe you're the same way and probably the other two as well. So if they did not kill her and there is no additional information why should we publicly humiliate important public servants? Nothing can be done for Bill. But the others, if their identities were made public, might find their careers in tatters. Their identities, if determined, would not further your case and would not exonerate my client. All it would do would be to embarrass three very important Dancing Deer men."

"And you're sure there is no additional information in the book?"

"Positive."

"Then keep it. I have to agree. However, I'll never be able to look at my fellow Dancing Deer brethren without wondering which one of them is Sugar Bear or Daddy Longlegs."

"You can restrict the possible candidates to only those who could afford a hundred dollars a month. That'll make it a lot easier and narrows the list of possible candidates down to a dozen or less."

"What else you got, counselor?"

"What do you know about Officer Henderson?"

"He's a capable officer. He was on the force when I got here four years ago. I have no reason to doubt his integrity."

"Who's responsible for the storage of property used in evidence?"

"He is."

"Okay, then let's discuss the gun found by Officer Henderson in Bill's glove box. I assume you told both officers to work together so a charge of planting evidence would have to include collusion."

"You bet I did."

"But Officer Henderson went straight to the garage while you and Bill made a pot of coffee in the kitchen."

"Yeah. After he came in with the gun I told him to work only with Officer McRae."

"Too late. But let's go on. I've traced the gun to Paul Nelson. He purchased it from Eberly's Sporting Goods five years ago."

"Now, how did you do that? The serial number's been filed off, there were no fingerprints, and that particular model's the most popular one sold."

"I know, but not with those oversized grips. He had to special order them." Jellico was enjoying this. "The gun was stolen from Mr. Nelson. He said he filed a report and when it was found on a suspect in an armed robbery it was held as evidence—with the serial number still intact. Then the man in charge of the evidence room finds the same gun in Bill's car while working alone and against his supervisor's explicit orders. So now, what can you tell me about Officer Henderson?"

"Damnit, Jellico. You're telling me I got a corrupt officer on my force. I'll have to get back to you."

"Okay, Chief. What have you got for me?"

"Counselor, the pillow's been found. There's a bullet hole in the center with powder burns all around and no blood or bone fragments. The city sanitation department found it in the trash of the retired junior high principal. She lives across the street from Bill. She doesn't have a car, has never heard of Raylene, or even been out of her house since last summer."

"Let's see, trash isn't picked up until Monday morning; you were scouring Bill's house Saturday morning. So Officer Henderson could have planted the pillow as well as the gun."

"If Henderson's involved, the rest of the force will see that he pays."

"Chief, if you feel about Raylene like Bill does then getting the real killer should be a lot more important to you than skewering Bill or protecting one of your own. Help me catch the real killer. If you find anything let me know, and I'll do the same with you."

CHAPTER 22—THE FUNERALS
February 22, 1945

Thursday morning at ten the downtown Presbyterian Church held Raylene's funeral. Much to the amazement of several attendees, Raylene was a regular member going two or three times per month. The minister told everyone she was the one who donated the piano. No mention was made of how she made her money. There were about thirty people in attendance including Daniel Poul's parents and Mrs. Carlisle, Raylene's mother. Jellico had sent Pepe and Harriet to Harrison to bring her back from the nursing home where she lived. They returned with a disoriented middle-aged woman and a positive report on the facility and its nursing attendants. Katy stood by the guest register and made every attendee sign in. She eventually turned the guestbook over to Jellico.

Raylene was as lovely as ever. When Thaddeus Wilke conducted the autopsy he took every precaution to not disfigure the body any more than necessary. He had a woman put on her makeup and another fix her hair. Several floral arrangements had been delivered and stood sentinel on both sides and behind the casket as a line of mourners passed by. Tears were shed as they gazed upon a truly beautiful woman and a good woman in spite of her circumstances.

When the line ended and most people were finding solace in quiet murmurings with their neighbor, two young men lowered the lid and arranged the covering wreath. When they walked away a lavish red rose bouquet lay across the top. With scented green tendrils interspersed with red rose buds and baby's breath, the arms of the bouquet spread around the curved lid as if they were hugging one of their own.

The service began when a friend from Raylene's prayer group walked to the piano and sang a beautiful rendition of *When me meet over there*. The minister's message was short and lyrical as he waxed over the goodness in Raylene's heart. Either he did not know about Raylene's occupation or had decided it was not important. The good things that surrounded Raylene, the good she accomplished, the good

111

she extracted from others, and the steadfast relationship she had with her creator more than compensated for any transgression. There was no need to hurl righteous indignation on someone so loved as Raylene Carlisle.

Special care was made to ensure none of the cards attached to the floral arrangements were lost. Jellico wanted a description of each arrangement and the attached card. Anyone touching any card had to wear gloves. He also made arrangements with the floral shops for their employees to be fingerprinted so those could be removed from the match-up file.

At the graveside, Jellico looked around to see if any latecomers arrived trying to bypass the register. They lowered Raylene into the ground and several people stepped forward to toss in a single red rose. One of those people was old man Ridley.

That afternoon Galen Hamelin's funeral was attended by a handful of mourners. Besides Jellico and his group the only others to show up were Sheriff Shodtoe, a couple of Snockered regulars, and Cody, the town vagrant. The service was held in the chapel of Mr. Wilke's funeral home. This time Harriet manned the guest register. After the short service Jellico asked Cody how he'd come to know Galen.

Trying to fathom Jellico's reason for asking, Cody answered, "He and I go back a long way. We're brothers."

"You're Mr. Hamelin's brother?"

"Well, not blood brothers. We had the same problems, tried to solve them the same way, and will no doubt come to the same end. I met him on the street and shared my shine. That makes us brothers in my eyes."

"You ever thought about giving up the drink?"

"Yeah. My old lady told me I could come home if I could stay away from the bottle. I've tried but the longest I've gotten was two weeks. My kids are growing up and I'm losing recollection of how they look."

"You're married? I've seen you sweep the streets and pick up trash but I never thought of you as a man with a family. How do you make the money you need to buy your booze?"

112

"I wash dishes, suck out grease pits, and ride the garbage wagon. Sometimes I do odd jobs for the elderly but I don't get money from them."

"If you really want to make the effort I might be able to offer some assistance. Is there any of those jobs you particularly like?"

"No."

"Okay. Have you got any other skills? What kind of work did you do before your wife kicked you out?"

"I taught school."

CHAPTER 23—THE TRIP
February 22, 1945

Pepe and Harriet headed to Harrison in Bill's Packard. Pepe was deep in thought while Harriet talked to him about how pretty the countryside was. It was early spring and daffodils had thrust yellow bursts of color from every ditch, hedgerow, and tended flower bed. Next would come tulips, then crocus'. Soon everyone would be planting a garden. Indeed, a few hardy souls had already planted seedlings nurtured in covered seed beds. With the soil temperature warming and the days gradually getting longer gardeners planted their seedlings in straight furrows under large glass bells.

"Pepe, you're not paying attention to anything I've been saying. What're you thinking about?"

"Harriet, honey, I've been wondering who'll take care of me when I can't take care of myself. Genevieve will be here in America, but without being able to speak the language I feel like an orphan. Back home I have my son but he wants to live a bohemian lifestyle in Paris. I have a large vineyard and produce two prestigious wines: a cabernet sauvignon and a merlot. They've won awards and, in a good year, I ship every bottle I can produce to customers around the world. I'm not hurting for money. So, I've been thinking about my prospects."

"Pepe, you're not old. You're still a handsome man and in good health. You cut a dashing figure, you're fun to be around; you're smart, witty, and charming. I think all you'll have to do is make it known you want companionship. They'll come out of the woodwork."

"What about you? Would you like to see France, travel to Switzerland, cruise the Mediterranean or the South Pacific?"

"If I thought I was completely over Bill I'd jump at the chance. Ask me again in a month, after the trial's over. You ever been to South America?"

"No. But I've always wanted to go to Rio for *Carnivale*."

"Me too."

From the back seat came a whisper. "I'd like to go."

Pepe looked over his shoulder at Mrs. Carlisle. "You'd like to go to Rio?"

She nodded. "If she won't go with you, come pick me up."

"Mrs. Carlisle, where'd you learn to speak French?"

"I lived in Quebec before marrying and moving south. Biggest mistake of my life."

"Mrs. Carlisle, what did you think of the funeral?"

"What funeral?"

"Harriet, I don't mean to alarm you, but a car has been following us since we left Dancing Deer."

"How do you know? We've only gone ten miles, maybe they'll turn off."

"They've been keeping the same distance. When I slow down they slow down—same for speeding up. Uh, oh. Here they come and we're next to a deep gully."

The car charged from behind and passed the Packard. It crossed back over the center stripe expecting to sideswipe the trio off the road. Pepe had anticipated the maneuver. As soon as the car started around, Pepe slammed on the brakes. When the car pulled back into Pepe's lane, instead of hitting the Packard's front left quarter panel and pushing Pepe and the two women down a steep ravine, it swished against vacant air.

Pepe gunned the Packard and easily overtook the older and slower Plymouth. Then the driver leaned out the window and fired a shot at the oncoming Packard. He didn't hit anything but made Pepe back off.

"Harriet, did you get the license plate number?"

"No, we never got close enough."

From the back seat came a soft, "Run his ass off the road."

"I think we'll keep our distance and see what he does. He'll need gas before long or he'll come to his destination. All we need's the license plate number."

In another minute the Plymouth made a u-turn in the highway and came back toward Pepe in the oncoming lane. "Ladies, lie down. He's going to shoot."

When the cars passed, all the driver of the Plymouth could see was a black Packard hurtling down the highway, void of occupants. He shot the back tire. Traveling at fifty, the Packard fishtailed when the tire blew, then left the road.

Mrs. Carlisle yelled, "Whoo-pee."

Harriet screamed. Pepe held the steering wheel in both hands and applied the brake liberally. "Hold on, ladies."

The Packard hit the ditch and turned over onto its side. It slid another twenty-five feet on the grass, coming to rest ten feet lower than the road and a fair distance away. The Plymouth turned around and came back to see if its prey had been successfully incapacitated. When it passed, the Packard was hidden below a sweeping curve as the road turned away from where the Packard had exited. Pepe jockeyed his car to a sliding stop while holding the steering in an iron grip. He was serenaded during the entire episode by two screaming women—one enjoying the ride.

From the highway the man driving the Plymouth didn't see the Packard lying on its side with the two skyward wheels still turning. He thought they were still ahead and, wanting to give it another try, he floored the Plymouth to catch up.

"Anybody hurt?"

"Not me."

From the back seat came, "Damned son-of-a-bitch."

"Mrs. Carlisle, are you okay?"

"Not really. I'm gonna sue."

Pepe rolled down his window and crawled out. "That's a damned fine automobile. I think if we can change the tire and get her righted she'll drive us right out of this."

Pepe walked to the back and popped open the trunk. He was in the process of taking out the spare tire when Harriet raised her head above the driver's side window. "Can I help?"

"Can you get out?"

"Maybe." Harriet struggled for a place to put her foot. She stuck it between the spokes of the steering wheel and, blowing the horn momentarily, she pulled herself up and through the window. Eventually she sat on the door jamb with her feet dangling free. "Whew. I made it, but I think Mrs. Carlisle will have to ride out righting the automobile from inside."

Pepe asked, "How do you think we can get it flipped onto its wheels?"

He lifted the tire out of the trunk and dropped it on the ground. He then retrieved the four-pronged spinner and climbed back onto the side of the car. While sitting on the back door Indian-style, he faced away from Harriet as he used the flat spoke to pry off the hubcap, then unscrewed the lug nuts, placing them in the hubcap. Ten minutes and he lifted the bad tire and threw it to the ground. Five minutes later he had manhandled the spare up and placed it on the axle. He then screwed on the lug nuts. He finished changing the tire by positioning the hubcap and stomping it into place.

On the ground he said to Harriet again, "How do you think we can get it flipped on its wheels?"

"I dunno."

Mrs. Carlisle lowered the driver's side back window and raised her head. "I think you ought to tie a rope on that bull and let him pull it over."

"You want to get me killed?" Pepe walked to the trunk of the car, threw in the bad tire, and retrieved a long coiled rope. "Got any ideas on how to get this around his neck?"

"Make a loop and lasso him."

"Like a cowboy?"

"Like Will Rogers."

Pepe walked to a nearby gate, unlatched it and walked into the pasture with the giant bull. When he got twenty feet away, the bull raised his head from the grass.

"Easy, boy. Damn, this is scary."

Pepe got as close as he thought safe and tossed the loop. It hit the bull on the side of the head and fell to the ground. Two more tries and two more failed efforts. Each time he tried, however, from a gradually shrinking distance—but not close enough. Finally he walked to a nearby tree, laid a big loop on the ground, tossed the rest of the coiled rope over a stout limb, and walked back to the car. From the trunk he retrieved the potted plant he'd given Mrs. Carlisle for her room.

"Mrs. Carlisle, may I have your corsage."

"You going to feed it to that beast?"

"I'm going to use it as bait."

With the carnation corsage and potted plant Pepe walked back into the pasture and placed both inside the rope loop with the corsage resting on top. He then carried the dangling portion of the rope toward another tree. Pepe picked up a long stick and walked behind the bull, swishing the stick on the ground. The bull raised his head and turned to see what Pepe might be doing. As Pepe got closer, the bull walked away a few feet, then a few feet farther, then close enough to the potted plant that his curiosity made him take a bite. The corsage fell to the ground. Pepe ran to the end of the rope and pulled it taut. The loop now encircled the bull's neck and he didn't like it one bit. The bull turned, pawed the ground, lowered his head, and ran at Pepe. When the bull had covered enough ground for the rope to stretch taut the animal yanked it free from Pepe's hand. For a man sixty-five years old Pepe was still pretty agile. He headed for the closest tree. He didn't think he could make it up, but with the bull quickly closing the gap he gave it his best effort. No luck. Pepe got on the other side of the tree and, as the bull circled, Pepe circled.

"Mister, you trying to rustle my bull?"

Harriet was sitting on the top board of the fence. "I told him I was in the mood for steak. He's French. They're always trying to please."

"Harriet, tell this man I only wanted his bull to help me upright the car."

"There's a stiff law for rustling a man's stock. Some people dispense with the legal aspects and handle matters themselves."

"Oh, posh. Can you help us get our car turned upright? We were run off the road and it flipped in the ditch. He wasn't trying to steal the cow; he just wanted some help righting the car."

The man looked past Harriet to the automobile. He then walked to the bull and removed the rope. "You two mosey on back to your car and I'll fetch the tractor. Be sure and close the gate. Here, take the rope." He started down a well-worn path, stopping only to say, "I thought sure you was going to make it up that tree."

CHAPTER 24—THE TRUST
February 23, 1945

The day after the funeral, Jellico went into the Marsden County Courthouse. He appeared in chambers with Judge Murphy McAdams.

"Your honor, Raylene Carlisle died intestate. She has assets of thirty thousand dollars in savings and checking, and a few hundred more in clothes and furnishings. Besides her mother, she has no living relative. The mother is in a convalescent home in Harrison suffering from dementia. I have prepared this paper to allow the First Bank and Trust of Dancing Deer to liquidate the assets and administer Raylene's funds on her mother's behalf. The funds will be used to pay the monthly charge for her mother's nursing care and room-and-board at the home and other incidental items she might need. Upon her mother's demise, the balance of the account will be donated to Miss Carlisle's church.

"I've made arrangements for a public accountant to audit the bank's record-keeping of her funds and to provide his opinion to the court on an annual basis. The charge is at his standard rate and will be paid from the estate." Jellico handed the judge a stapled document of three pages from his briefcase.

"I agree, Mr. Jellico, and applaud your penchant for detail. You may take immediate action in the matter. What's your fee?"

"Nothing, your honor."

"Very benevolent, Mr. Jellico. What fee will the bank be charging for the administration of the trust?"

"Again, nothing, your honor."

"Have you contacted the convalescent home? I'd hate to think the wheels of justice turn so slowly that Miss Carlisle's mother has been placed in a state ward for lack of payment."

"I have, your honor. I had two of my colleagues bring her in for Raylene's funeral. They took her back immediately afterwards. When they picked her up they found that the only other funds she might need were for outings and activities. Also, there is a canteen where she can buy magazines, makeup, and similar types of items. I have included monthly funds to allow her spending money and to continue her weekly visit to the salon where she gets her hair fixed."

"Thank you Mr. Jellico. See you in court."

Jellico snapped shut his briefcase, shook hands with Judge McAdams, and headed back to his office. He thought how different it was handling the paperwork versus strategizing a murder trial. He had a lot of experience filing briefs, researching county records, preparing wills, planning estates, and so on but no experience whatsoever in saving a man's life from the clutches of a salivating district attorney—of a district attorney wanting to use the trial to catapult him into the governor's mansion.

As Jellico walked the few blocks to his office several people nodded, greeted him with a hearty good morning, or simply smiled. Suddenly it dawned on Jellico why the people in the town were so friendly when they had not been before. It wasn't like they had been rude or anything but they normally treated him like he was just another person on the sidewalk and not anyone of a particular note. But now he was a celebrity.

And the number two reason, Jellico thought, for their changed disposition had to do with life's changing circumstances. One day a normal person is going about his business oblivious to civil injustices perpetrated on his fellow man and the next he is that man being scrutinized by the legal system. We are a litigious society and people sometimes need a good lawyer so that they can keep what they've got, keep the big bad wolf from blowing their house down, and keep themselves right with the law. The people in Dancing Deer must be reasoning that, if Bill Potter would trust his life to Michael Jellico, then this Jellico might be able to help them should the occasion arise. Jellico stood a bit more upright, his shoulders carrying a little more weight, and his sense of self worth at an all-time high.

CHAPTER 25—VOIR DIRE

"Bill, you separated the good from the bad? We can remove six, the prosecution gets six, and the judge gets six of his own. We got to pick out the worst six and convince the state that our next group of six is really their group. And then we gotta show the judge that six of our other bad jurors are so bad he'll have to throw them out to keep from stinking up the jury pool. Then he'll randomly select twelve of those left and six alternates. So which are our first six?"

Bill handed Jellico a stack of paper with the worst potential jurors separated and placed on top. These were the people most wanting to see him fry in the chair everyone called "Old Spanky." The bailiff brought the first prospective juror forward to the witness stand and swore him in. Jellico found his sheet and walked forward. "Mr. Smyth, do you have any preconceived opinions as to the guilt or innocence of Bill Potter?"

"No, sir."

"Mr. Smyth, do you have a bank account at the First Bank and Trust of Dancing Deer?"

"No, sir. I use the bank in Skunk Hollow."

"That's fifteen miles away. Is there any reason why you don't use the local bank?"

"I just think my money's safer there."

"I see. Have you ever applied for a loan at the Dancing Deer bank, Mr. Smyth?"

"Yeah."

"And been turned down?"

"No. I was loaned the money. Put the farm up as collateral. When the economy went bust Mr. Potter came out himself and told me I had thirty days to move my family from our farm. My great-grandfather homesteaded it, built the house by hand from logs he cut from his own

123

stand of timber. Three months later Potter sold it to a man from Moccasin Gap for a song. Said I owed the bank the remaining balance."

"Your honor, may I approach?"

"Approach, counselor."

Standing beside Emmett Irving, Jellico said, "Your Honor, every one of these prospective jurors has a biased opinion. Either their dealings with Bill's bank helped them in some way and they have a positive opinion of his worth and collaterally of his innocence or they were turned down for a loan, had their farm or home foreclosed on, or they feel oppressed in some other way by the most important man of finance in our town."

"Counselor, are you asking for a change in venue?"

"Under the circumstances, your honor, I think it's our only alternative."

"Mr. Irving, does the state have an observation to give the court?"

"No, your honor. I'm only interested in a fair trial. However, we have eighty prospective jurors. I'm sure, with due diligence, Mr. Jellico and I can find eighteen who can offer an un-biased assessment of Mr. Potter's innocence or guilt."

"Mr. Jellico, would Wind Springs be a suitable choice for an alternative venue?"

"May I confer with my client, your honor?"

The judge brought down his gavel and in a booming voice said, "This court is in recess. We will reconvene at ten o'clock. Counselors, in my chambers in thirty minutes."

"Bill, we can't get a fair trial here. Every one of these people has something against you. Hell, Smyth was in your good stack. How could a man make so many enemies? The judge said he could move it to Wind Springs. We'll rent several rooms at the Piccadilly Hotel and . . ."

"Jellico, Wind Springs won't work. Any town in America except Wind Springs. I busted up three hoodlums with a two-by-four there three months ago. They turned out to be the boys of the town's chief of police."

"Damnit, Bill, you never cease to amaze me." Jellico sat in the chair beside Bill and started looking through the sheets of notebook paper. "I'm doubling my fee."

In the judge's chambers, Jellico said, "Your honor, Bill wants to take his chances with the people in his home town. He has faith in the justice system and, although he's been rough on several citizens, he's also been fair. That's all he wants from them, for them to be fair with him."

"Very well. We'll reconvene in fifteen minutes."

Emmett Irving turned to Chief Wainwright and whispered, "That's hogwash. Send someone to Wind Springs and find out why Bill doesn't want the trial to go there."

By Friday the prospective jurors had been questioned by both the prosecuting and defense attorneys. Jellico asked for six to be removed, Emmett wanted one removed, and the judge removed six for cause.

CHAPTER 26—THE TUCKER FARM

"Harriet, are you going to be okay?"

"They're locked up, aren't they? And we'll be in a supervised area, won't we?"

"I hope so. The prisons in France and those run by the Gestapo wouldn't be places a pretty woman like you would be safe under any circumstance. If it looks like the guards won't be able to provide adequate protection I think we should leave. I'll come back on the weekend with Jellico."

"Pepe, you're so sweet. I'll be okay."

"And you know what to ask and what to divulge."

"Yes. We've been over it a dozen times. It still astonishes me how you were able to figure it out."

"It all started with the bus fares for different amounts. Then there were the two savings accounts. The rifling of Raylene's apartment, and Daniel's parents at her funeral. This has to be the answer."

"Still, the rest of us had the same clues and couldn't link them together. I think you're so smart, Pepe. And I'm plenty smart for seeing that in you. Somehow I knew you were the one to figure it all out." Harriet leaned over and kissed Pepe on the cheek.

Pepe put his hand on Harriet's. "In France we say you should kiss those who pleasure you and pleasure those who kiss you."

Inside the prison Harriet and Pepe signed in and were led to a room partitioned with a waist-high wall and screened from there to the ceiling. There was no way a visitor could sneak something to the inmate he was visiting. In a few minutes Daniel Poul was led into the room. He sat in a chair on his side of the partition expecting someone to come in he'd recognize. Pepe and Harriet walked over and sat on the opposite side.

"Mr. Poul, I'm Harriet and this is Pepe. We work for Bill Potter's defense lawyer. I'm sorry to have to tell you that Raylene's been murdered."

"Yes, I know. My father wrote me a letter telling me that our illustrious banker is being tried for the crime. I knew she was a prostitute but I didn't care. I loved Raylene. I didn't pay her any money. We just had good times together. I hope they fry your Bill Potter."

"Do you hope they fry Bill Potter or they fry Raylene's killer?"

"What? You don't think Potter did it?"

"No, we think you did it."

"Me? Lady, you two are crazy. I've been locked up here for seven years."

"I understand. But let's review the facts. First of all, we're not the police. Nothing you say to us will harm you in any way. If Bill Potter actually killed Raylene then he should die, but if it was someone else then that other person should die instead. We just have to piece the puzzle together and find out exactly who the murderer was. Are you with me so far?"

"Sure. But you're wasting my . . . your time. I've got plenty of time to waste."

"Okay. Let's review what Pepe, my detective friend, has put together and get your assessment of its credibility. First of all, Raylene had regular clients on most week nights and was seeing you on weekends. When your next door neighbor died you ransacked her house and took the pile of money you found to Raylene for safekeeping."

"You have no way of proving that."

"Raylene's apartment was torn completely apart. The murderer was looking for something. The only thing she had of any value was the money you told her to keep. No one knew about the money except for the dead woman who saved it, you, and Raylene. So how did the murderer know about it? You had to mention it in here."

"I did not."

"Then you either talk in your sleep or it's written down in your things and your cell mate found it."

"I have to think." Daniel put his head in his hands. "Did they find any money when they tore up Raylene's apartment?"

"We don't know. There was no cash money found by the police or by us."

"Damn. Then that's that." Daniel got up from his chair and paced the floor, thinking. In a short while he sat back down. "I gave Raylene ten thousand dollars in fifties and hundreds. She didn't know where it came from. Of course she eventually figured it out when I was tried for its theft. She wrote me letters once a month for the first couple of years and she came to see me on weekends. Then it was every other month for a few years and just twice this last year. I wrote her every day until a couple of years ago when she asked me to stop.

"She said she still had the money but spent the biggest portion of her time while here trying to convince me to give it back. I told her I wouldn't, that the money was for us to move somewhere and start a new life together. That's when she told me she didn't love me, that she didn't love anyone—couldn't love anyone. I didn't understand—still don't. Anyway, I kept the letters. So I guess someone could have read them when I had a work detail.

"My cellies would've been the only ones with access. When my old cellie walked out his wife and kids were waiting, and he swore he'd never do anything to ever hurt them again. But my cellie now is a different story. He's the devil himself."

"What's his name?"

"Gleason Bonds."

"Do you know if he's had any visitors?"

"Yeah. His brother Evan comes by once in a while. He lives in Wind Springs."

"Daniel, would you give the money back if it meant an early parole?"

"I thought you said she didn't have the money."

"She didn't have any cash money, but she did have a savings account with ten thousand and some interest in it."

"Well, that's my money and you tricked me."

"Mr. Poul, we had no way of knowing that her savings was actually your money. We can only surmise now because the two amounts are the same. So what do you say? Do you want out early?"

"It wouldn't be too early. I'm due for review in five months."

"Let's consider these facts. Raylene died intestate. She didn't have a will. All of her money's been turned over to the court and is now being used by them to take care of her only living relative. So if Raylene still had your money, when you walk out in five months you couldn't get to it. But if you tell the court about it and walk out in a couple of weeks, you still won't have your money but you will have your freedom and five months of your life back."

"When you put it like that I have to take what I can. Get me outta here. I'll do whatever you want."

"Okay, but don't say anything to Mr. Bonds. We don't want him tipping off his brother, convincing Evan to go underground."

CHAPTER 27—THE ABDUCTION

Evan sat low in the car. He'd been watching the house for two days and nights. Potter drove here after leaving Raylene Carlisle's apartment and parked his car in the garage. This was his house, had to be. Evan thought the other couple he watched come and go were Potter's relatives. They all lived in the same house. But, for the past two days he'd been here, Potter hadn't been around.

He could've handled Potter that first night, but after screwing up stealing Raylene's money he'd decided he should think about it. Two mistakes in one night might be one too many. He'd stuffed the pillow in the trash can across the street. He felt sure the police would find it and think Potter discarded it there. That and the witness seeing Potter leave the scene were probably enough to get the man charged with murder. Evan knew his dad would've been able to add the pieces together. After a week passed and Potter was actually charged, Evan decided Potter could now be dispensed with. Show him not to mess with the Bonds boys. To the police it would look like vigilante justice: a friend or relative retaliating against some wealthy dude before he bought his way off. The first attempt had failed. He'd not been prepared for a pregnant woman with a stick. His shoulder was still swollen and with a puncture wound that had become infected. He needed to see a doctor, but not here.

Then he tried to push Potter off the road. Hell, what a fiasco. He hadn't gone down the road another ten miles before that deputy sheriff pulled him over for speeding. Caught doing ninety in a thirty-five—leaving him broke and Potter still puttering around town. What's with that Victory Speed anyway? Before the war the limit was much higher. Evan decided he needed to go back to Wind Springs, get his shoulder doctored, and steal some working capital from his old man. He'd take a couple of weeks off and lick his wounds.

A month later Evan decided it was time. He'd start off by paying one more visit to Raylene's apartment. There wasn't mention in the paper of any money being found. Maybe it was still there. The cops weren't looking for it specifically, just clues in general.

It was night. Evan parked the green Plymouth two blocks away and walked to Raylene's apartment building. Staying in the shadows, when Evan had determined no one was watching he used Raylene's key to go in the back way. That was awful smart. Take her keys. Besides no money being found, there was also no mention in the paper about her keys being missing. These guys must not be as smart as his old man. He'd have caught that in ten minutes.

Evan thought he better be organized about this. Pull the shades down, close the curtains, one lamp on a long cord and shade off. Hell, this was easy. Now if he were a broad with money to hide . . . hmm. Let's see . . . he'd take it one room at a time. Do the closets first. Evan checked the clothes and dragged everything off the shelves above the clothes. Nothing. Bathroom. That's the most likely place anyway. Walking from the hall closet, he noticed something different about the desk. Evan ran to it. The center drawer was shoved in crooked. This was the first place he'd looked. A few pictures, some books, and a bank register showing a balance of a measly seventy-six dollars. They're gone. Books still here but everything else gone. Must be evidence. Evan shoved the drawer back in. That's screwy; the drawer won't shut all the way. Evan got down on his knees and looked under the desk. Aw, hell, this is where she had the money and someone's already found it. At the back of the drawer, a secret compartment. Damn French. Build something like that.

Bet that Bill Potter found my money. I think I'll call him up and tell him I want it. Give him something back in return, like his mother. At that moment Evan had a bright idea. Hey, what about that tall redhead. He'd pay through the nose if someone kidnapped her. Evan knew the tall redhead worked at the paper. He also knew she worked late on Friday nights helping to get Saturday's edition run. It was a semi-weekly paper, put out on Wednesdays and Saturdays. She walked home sometime between ten and twelve every Tuesday and Friday nights. This was made to order. Evan parked in an alleyway a block from the newspaper. She'd have to walk right by.

Faye enjoyed working with the pressman. He did all the work, only telling her to flip the switch every once in a while or yelling for more ink. She liked to listen to the rollers whir and the mechanical gears gnash. It was exciting after spending the earlier part of the day setting type. She loved writing the articles, but this was a big part of the newspaper business as well and exhilarating in its own way.

"Miss Spencer, I got it from here. Just got to cut and fold. You go on home."

"Thanks Ivan. It's been a long day. You want me to bring you anything before I go?"

"No. I'm fine. I'm not like you. I get my entire week done two evenings each week, one before each edition. You'll have to be back Monday morning."

"It's all right, Ivan. Today Jesse told me to start coming in late the days after I help you the night before. Tuesdays and Fridays now begin at noon. But if you're sure you can handle it from here then I'll go."

Ivan looked up from tinkering with a set of gears. He made a motion with his hand for her to go.

"See ya next week." Faye grabbed her coat and threw a wool scarf around her neck. Her apartment building was nine blocks from the newspaper. It took fifteen minutes unless she dallied. No dallying tonight. Too blooming cold. One block from the newspaper, a hand reached out from a dark alleyway grabbing her arm.

"I've got a gun. No screaming and you won't get hurt."

Faye froze. She tried to raise her hands but he yanked her toward the alley. "Please, mister. You can have my money. I've got more than twenty dollars. Take it, jewelry too."

"Shut up. You don't give me no problem you ain't going to get hurt. I'm going to sell you to Potter."

Evan reached in his back pocket and pulled out a pair of his dad's handcuffs. With a practiced ease, he fastened them on Faye's wrists behind her back and shoved her into the Plymouth.

"What are you going to do to me?"

"I'm going to slap you silly if you keep yapping."

Evan drove to the Ghent Building and parked in the small parking area behind. He showed Faye his gun, then pushed her toward the heavy back door. After pulling open the door, he shoved her inside and pulled the door shut. With a new flashlight he found the light switch and turned it on. Faye now saw her assailant.

"You're just a boy. How old are you?"

"I'm plenty old enough to take care of you. Don't mess with me and you'll be okay. Your boyfriend's got my money. As soon as he gives it back you're free to go. In the meantime, stay calm and don't cause no problems."

"Okay. You got his number? Let's get this over with."

Evan marched Faye up the stairs. When they stepped onto the second floor Evan turned on an overhead light. "There's no windows up here and the walls are a foot thick. Used to be a bank. You get that back room and I'll stay out here. Your door locks from the inside. Keep it locked if you want. Don't open it unless I tell you to. You got that? You got to ask before you open that door. Here's a folding chair. Lots of 'em stacked beside the courthouse annex. You'll have to sleep in your coat. If we're still here tomorrow night, I'll get you a quilt or something. Now, what's his number?"

CHAPTER 28—THE RANSOM

Saturday morning Katy called Bill. "I'm worried sick. Faye didn't come home last night. She works late on Tuesday and Friday nights but she's always home by midnight."

"Have you called the police?"

"Not yet. I was hoping she was staying the night with you."

"That's not happened yet. I suggest you call the police. Have you talked with any of the others? I think it's time we had another pow-wow."

"After I talk to the police I'll call Jellico and see what he thinks."

"Katy, there's probably some logical explanation. Maybe that French private eye has some ideas. He used to follow her around until he gave up on her learning any of his language. Get back to me if you hear of anything or if Jellico wants to bring everyone up to date."

Later that morning the telephone rang again, "Is this Bill Potter?"

"Yes, I'm Bill Potter."

"The Bill Potter who killed that woman and gent?"

"Is this a prank? You can get whatever information you need from the newspaper. Goodbye."

"No. Wait a minute. Don't hang up. I've got something you want."

"Yeah? What would that be?"

"Your girl." Evan waited. After receiving no response he continued, "The tall redhead, the one who works for the paper. I got her tied to a chair."

"What do you want?"

"Money. Thirty thousand dollars or you'll never see her again."

135

"I haven't got thirty thousand. The state took all my money when I posted bail. Can I give you something else? You want title to my Packard? I've got some jewelry . . . paintings."

"I want your money." Evan thought he'd better back down a bit. He didn't want to kill the woman. "I'll give you a few days. Better sell that jewelry. And that car . . . I thought I run you off the road in that car. Don't bring no one else into this. If I find out you've told anyone, she's dead."

"Is there any way you can assure me she's not already dead? May I talk with her?"

"No. I can't get her to a telephone. Give me a question. When I call you back I'll give you her answer."

"Okay. Ask her what famous book heroine she's thought to look like."

"You got it. Now, start getting that money together. I'll get back to you on Monday."

Evan stopped at the diner on the way back. He got two chicken salad sandwiches to go and a couple bottles of soda. When he arrived at the empty bank, he hurried up the stairs.

"I'm back. Did you miss me?"

"Get these handcuffs off me. You creep, you think you can hang me up like a side of beef?"

"Calm down. I can't lock you up. All the rooms lock from the inside and I ain't got a key to the back door. You think I'm going to just let you walk out while I'm calling that guy of yours?"

"Is he going to pay you your money?"

"Said he didn't have it. For me to go ahead and shoot you."

"You're lying. Let me talk to him. I'll get you your money."

"Relax. I got it covered. He wants you to answer a question so he'll know you're still alive. Anybody ever say you looked like someone in a book?"

"Yes. Helen, in Homer's *Iliad*. Tell him Helen."

"Okay, let's get some rules made. If you'll stay in your room and not sneak out, then I'll leave the handcuffs off—except when I'm gone. In return I'll get you whatever you want to make your stay comfortable. I'll also promise not to hurt you."

136

"I'll make you a list."

Evan took Faye's money and went to the Dancing Deer Mercantile. He bought two lawn chairs that reclined, two sleeping bags, six pads of paper and six pens, a chamber pot, and a large water jug. On the way back he stopped at a grocery store and purchased a sack of food and a pie pan. He got crackers, bread, cookies, and small tins—some of vienna sausages and others of sardines. At the last minute he added a toothbrush and a tube of toothpaste.

Faye took the items purchased and locked the door. Bill would come up with that money and she'd be out of there. In the meantime she'd write a book. She spent two hours deciding what to write about. A fictional account of the murder. How it could have happened. She'd name it *Murder on my Doorstep* or maybe, *Murder in Dancing Deer.*"

Sunday morning Evan awoke to the back door opening. He'd been sleeping in the large room outside the woman's cell. Holding the gun like a flashlight, he crept down the dark stairs.

"Harold, I'll make you a great deal. I need the money, so I'm willing to take a loss. Give me thirty thousand and she's all yours."

"Bill, you paid forty-five thousand two weeks ago. Why do you want to unload it so soon for such a big loss?"

"With this trial starting tomorrow, Jellico says I need to pay him part of his fee. And I've got two detectives scouring Dancing Deer for proof I'm innocent. I'll make it all back when the trial's behind me. I had to purchase it to run those goof-offs from Skunk Hollow out of town."

"I dunno. It's awfully dark in here. The Ghents were so afraid someone was going to rob the place that they built it without any windows."

Evan waited on Bill Potter and his prospective purchaser to walk past the staircase then he crept to the bottom and followed from behind. In his stocking feet, walking on the slick hardwoods, and carrying a gun he was a cat stalking prey.

Harold Greenleaf said, "If I were to put a corridor down the center and build out offices I might be able to rent it to a lawyer or two. What do you think?"

"I think that would be wonderful. There's hardly any office space for rent. You'll make a killing."

"I think I've seen enough. Let's go see the brickwork. I won't buy it for sure if I have to make structural repairs."

The two men started walking to the back door. Evan didn't have time to make it to the stairs. There weren't any closets. He quickly surveyed the area and stepped inside the safe. He'd pull the door almost shut—leaving an inch or so. If they found him he'd shoot 'em and if they didn't find him he'd have his thirty thousand when they made the deal. The door was heavy. It took both hands and lots of body leverage to get it moving.

The First Law of Motion, made famous by Sir Isaac Newton, is that every object in a state of uniform motion tends to remain in that state of motion unless an external force is applied. The door started moving—a uniform motion. When it neared the metal jam Evan started applying the brakes—an external force. The weight was too much, causing the movement to be too powerful, and the external force—clad in socks—too puny. Evan couldn't stop the door. It closed, sliding Evan into the recesses of a steel coffin. "Click."

"What was that sound?" Harold asked.

"I didn't hear any sound, Harold."

"Bill, I think I'll have to pass. You either got ghosts or rats."

"How about twenty-five thousand? I really need to sell today."

"Bill, you got me afraid. I'm not interested at any price. I think I'll walk. See you later."

Bill slowly made it out the back door. He turned the key in the lock and trudged toward the hotel. "Damn. Damn. Damn."

CHAPTER 29—THE UPDATE

Sunday evening Sherman Shodtoe opened his door for the second co-conspirator. Raymond Henderson returned earlier in the day from Wind Springs and, calling his cousin, Sheriff Shodtoe, said they needed to talk.

"Come on in, Ray. Care for a beer?"

"Yeah. You're not gonna believe what I found out."

The three men huddled around Sherman's dinette. Besides the sheriff and Officer Henderson, there was Deputy Rafe, or maybe Ralph, Johnson. Both leaned forward to hear what Ray had found.

"Potter and Jed Calhoun were tracking down Potter's daughter when they stopped to eat at this diner in Wind Springs. Three young toughs decided Potter had parked his car in their space and proceeded to shove it back into the street. Potter saw what was happening, came out of the diner, and beat the crap out of all three. Somewhere he found a stick and used it with authority. The youngest was husky and about twenty. Potter put him in the hospital. Rearranged his manhood . . . what I was told was that Potter smashed his balls flat. They had to do an operation. Now that guy sings soprano."

"Wow. That Bill Potter is something."

"Yeah. I heard he never took off his jacket—never raised a sweat."

Sherman Shodtoe had a big smile on his face. "I do believe Bill's gonna get himself removed from my list. I kinda like his style. What did you find out about the license plate?"

"Wait. The story's not over. With the youngest in the hospital, the other two go off and rob a Chinese laundry. But instead of politely giving them his money, this little feller pulls a gun, shoots one, and captures the other. His wife calls the police. And guess who shows up? The chief of police is Benjamin Bonds, their dad. He comes charging down the street with his siren wailing to find it was his two boys who robbed the laundry. The one still alive is now doing time at the Tucker Farm. And that green Plymouth is registered to the chief. I figure the youngest son came looking for Bill when he got released from the hospital."

There was considerable laughter as they tried to reconstruct the events in their minds. Rafe, or Ralph, asked, "How did he do it? Smash the man's, you know, his testicles?"

"The waitress told me that with two on the ground writhing in pain, Bill backed the last one against his car, whispered something in his ear, and used the butt-end of the stick like an underhanded hammer thrust to pulverize whatever might be hanging. He left all three lying in the parking lot. The youngest holding his feet high in the air shaking." Ray took a big swig of beer. "They got that piece of two by four mounted on the wall behind the cash register."

Everyone listening laughed. Henderson would have to repeat the entire story again to the men at police headquarters and write his report. He'd have them rolling on the floor.

"I got the money." Sherman walked to the bedroom, returning shortly with three envelopes. He handed an envelope to each man and decided to keep the third until the second twin asked for it. He knew if he gave it to Rafe, or maybe Ralph, his brother would never get payment.

Bill was despondent. He had not been able to sell the Ghent building and didn't have the funds to pay Faye's ransom. He looked in turn at each guest. They were seated around his dining room table, waiting to inform everyone else how productive their sleuthing had been. Jellico started things off with the tracking of the gun and then the pillow. Harriet said how she and Pepe were shot at by a man in a green Plymouth and then run off the road.

"Did you see his face?"

"No, Pepe said he was going to shoot so we ducked as the two cars passed. The man driving the Plymouth shot our back tire and then we run off the road and turned over."

"Was anyone hurt?"

"No. Not even Mrs. Carlisle."

Jellico jumped up. "I'll bet that bullet is still in the tire. We've got to get it."

Harriet said something to Pepe. He reached into his breast pocket and pulled out a small silk purse with drawstrings pulled tight. He handed it to Jellico. Opened and turned upside down on the table, the purse gave up its cargo of lead.

Harriet said, "Pepe thinks it's a .38 caliber slug."

"It's some help, but until someone finds the slug that killed Hamelin and ballistics can compare the two, it's just another loose end." Jellico sat down.

"I got a call Saturday afternoon from the man who ran you off the road." Bill adjusted his chair and started wringing his hands. "He says he's got Faye and wants thirty thousand dollars."

There was a collective gasp. "I spent Saturday and Sunday trying to come up with that much money. He told me if I told anyone he'd kill her. But I only have ten thousand. I've been buying a lot of property lately and, with the bank examiners looking at the bank's books, I'll have to go through the normal procedures and make a loan using some of that new property as collateral. With all the hoops in place, it'll be the end of next week before I'll have the money."

Katy shouted, "I'll pay the thirty thousand." She realized how loud she spoke and at a more modest level said, "I was wondering what to do with my money."

Bill continued, "He's supposed to call Monday. I guess we can meet here again after tomorrow's theatrics and wait for his call."

Pepe escorted Harriet to her room and, after not being invited in, continued to his room for another night sans female companionship.

Harriet called Bill. "I'd like to come back to the penthouse and get your answers to Pepe's questions."

"Sure. I'll leave the elevator in its free status. Would you like for me to have the kitchen prepare anything?"

"They got something laced with chocolate?"

Ten minutes later Harriet stepped off the elevator into Bill's living room. He was at the bar mixing something in a large glass tumbler. "You still drink martinis?"

"Oh, that's wonderful. You got olive juice to add?"

Bill reached into the small icebox next to the bar and retrieved a jar of olives. He poured from the bottle directly into the tumbler and stirred with a glass stick. He then poured two drinks into wide-brimmed stemware and dropped olives stuck on toothpicks in each.

"Here you are. One fantastic martini—dirty."

"Willie, let's go onto the balcony."

It was early April and, interspersed between cold spells, an occasional warm day or evening wandered in. Tonight was brisk but not requiring a coat. They sat on thick cushions in wrought iron chairs. From the fourth floor they had a view of the little town of Dancing Deer. Not much happening at eight o'clock on a Sunday evening.

Harriet took a notebook and pen from her purse. "Willie, do you know why Jennifer quit? She's listed as a witness for the prosecution."

"Not really. She'd worked for me for a number of years and then said she couldn't take it any more. She gave me a two-week notice and I haven't seen her since."

"She says you killed a man by putting him in an unhealthy situation."

"I had to have him moved. Jed was looking for him and I didn't want him found. Jennifer helped me find another old-folks home and set up his transfer. But I've now owned up to that dreadful business and received forgiveness from Jed."

"Did you ever drink beer at Raylene's?"

"Sometimes, during summer months."

"Where did you park your car when you visited Raylene?"

"Two blocks away on Main Street. However, on the night of the murder I had planned to stay only a minute or so and parked in front of the apartment building next door."

"Did Raylene own a gun?"

"Not that I know."

Harriet put the notebook and pen in her purse and sipped the martini. She looked down onto Main Street. An occasional car drove by and things seemed so peaceful. It was hard for her to imagine a murder in this quiet little town. Bill got up and went inside. In a moment he reappeared with the tumbler and poured another round of drinks.

"Willie, where do you think we went wrong? We were so much in love in the beginning. I've spent countless hours trying to get a grasp on my shortcomings."

"I think you might have been in love with love. It's what every girl thinks of. Their Prince Charming sweeping them off their feet and carrying them over a bed of rose petals to a castle. For me, I wanted the sex. When you got pregnant I did what every honorable man would do and even those not so honorable when the father of the pregnant girl shows up with a shotgun."

"My father did that?"

"He wasn't carrying a shotgun, but he did come by for a talk."

Harriet ate an olive and used the toothpick to stir her drink. "So you never loved me?"

"I moved into your parent's house—into your bedroom. I developed a routine. Study all day and night, only taking time off for classes and regular sex. I soon found I liked making the good grades, having other students ask me to explain difficult concepts, and having my papers read aloud in class. And the sex was wonderful. I think I gradually fell in love with you."

"That's reassuring."

"After graduation I received several job offers but nothing seemed worthy of all the effort I had put forth, and then Dad died. The rose-petal path you wanted turned out to be the rail line and the castle was an average house in a little town where nothing much was happening."

"I remember. I was bored stiff."

"You stayed a month. When you left you wrote a note saying 'I'm outta here.'"

"Willie, do you think Jed forgave you because you asked him or because you showed him you were truly sorry. And if he forgave you, would it be possible for you to forgive me?"

"I forgave you years ago."

"You never said anything. How was I to know?"

"We both had to get on with our lives. This was where I belonged. My parents, my grandparents, and even their parents lived here. I visit their graves sometimes. It's the same with you except your family was in Boston. Unless one of us was willing to step outside our world and enter the other's, we couldn't have had a successful relationship."

"I'm willing. I miss you, Willie. There hasn't been anyone else since I left. I went to lots of parties, was in my girlfriends' weddings, and went out on dates, but I always compared the available men with you and woke up in an empty bed."

"Harriet, I love Faye."

Harriet drank the rest of her martini, picked up her purse, and ran to the elevator. She descended past her floor to Pepe's. Walking down the hallway, deep in thought, and with tears flowing, she was overtaken by the waitress from the bistro. Harriet slowed her pace as the waitress reached Pepe's door and knocked. In a moment the young lady was whisked inside. Harriet turned around. She spent the rest of the night crawling out of a hole of self-pity and then planning her return to princesshood. She eventually convinced herself all was not yet lost. Interested parties should beware of a conniving woman.

CHAPTER 30—OPENING STATEMENTS

Chief Wainwright caught Jellico on the courthouse steps. "About two months ago I got a call from Raylene on a Thursday night. She wanted me to come over for the evening. I was pretty excited and rapped on her apartment door, holding a sack of clean clothes, not more than thirty minutes later. She said Sheriff Shodtoe had tried to shake her down. He lived across the street and figured out what she did when he noticed the same men sneaking in the back door with their hats pulled low. She said she called him a bad name and slammed the door in his face."

Jellico looked down, pensively pondering this new twist.

"And I've found that Officer Henderson is Shodtoe's cousin. Just thought you'd like to know."

"Any possibility of getting a warrant to search Shodtoe's apartment?"

"If you can get me something I can show the judge. He'll not go for opinions. See you in court, counselor."

Jellico walked down the long corridor. Lots more people wanted in to watch the show than the courtroom could hold. Sheriff Shodtoe and his two deputies were trying to keep order. It was also their responsibility to escort called witnesses to be questioned. Outside the courtroom they had to keep the witnesses separated so their testimony would not be tainted with information gleaned by another witness conversing with a neighbor.

Jellico was having second thoughts about his ability to get Bill off the hook. So far the prosecution had not even considered making a deal and Bill continued to deny his complicity. When Jellico entered the halls of justice, he saw Bill seated at the defense table. Jellico had had the presence of mind to tell Bill to come two hours early so he wouldn't get mobbed by well-wishers or hecklers.

What the hell? Bill had red lipstick emblazoned on his forehead. "How you feeling, Bill? You up to this?"

"I'm ready, Jellico. What about our case? They got enough evidence that I should be worried?"

"Absolutely. Anything can happen. But we've only got to convince one juror. One obstinate person who knows deep down you didn't do it." Jellico paused a moment and then said, "Bill, keep an eye on that door to your left. Let me know when the bailiff enters." With Bill looking to an unpopulated area of the courtroom, Jellico continued, "While the Emmett is giving his opening statement you look directly at each juror. Try to make eye contact. Then when I get up to talk in your defense, turn away from the jury and read from any of these papers." Jellico opened his worn briefcase and removed a sheaf of papers.

The courtroom filled to capacity. In a few minutes the bailiff came in and had everyone stand as the judge walked in from a second side door. After a few preliminaries Emmett Irving slowly got to his feet and stretched as if he'd been sitting for hours. A tall skinny guy who liked a show better than most, Jellico thought he probably considered this trial his ticket to the governor's mansion.

"Ladies and gentlemen of the jury, I come here to ask your help." Emmett surveyed the jurors. They were all smiling. "The state thinks . . . no, the state knows, Bill Potter smothered his lover, Raylene Carlisle, and shot Galen Hamelin in a cold, calculated, and gruesome manner." He paused and walked to the other end of the seated jurors.

"We'll prove, beyond a shadow of a doubt, that Bill Potter had an argument with Mr. Hamelin." Emmett looked straight at one of the jurors. "That Potter was robbed by Mr. Hamelin. That later, he shot Hamelin and retrieved his lost loot."

Emmett tried to lock eyes with another juror. No one was looking at him. They're all looking at the defense table. They're all smiling. Somewhat unnerved Emmett continued, "The night of the murder was his night. He spent every Friday night with Miss Carlisle. A witness puts him there. Moreover, Potter acknowledges he actually was there. So Potter had the motive, the opportunity, and, with the discovery of the suspected murder weapon in his car, the means.

"The first thing you learn when trying to come up through the ranks is that to solve a crime you have to follow the money trail. We have Potter winning all Mr. Hamelin's money. Mr. Hamelin making Potter give it back outside, and the money disappearing from Hamelin's pocket after being shot. We have Potter paying for Miss Carlisle's apartment, him wanting to break off the relationship, and her threatening to make it public unless he continued to pay up. The state thinks, and I think you'll agree, the money trail starts with Bill Potter and ends with Bill Potter.

"I said I need your help. But it's more than that. It's your civic duty to weigh the evidence and, when the smoke's cleared and Bill Potter stands before you with blood on his hands, to shout as one 'You're guilty as sin.'"

Emmett turned away from the jury and walked toward his seat. He looked at Bill. Instead of sitting down, he walked over to Bill and asked, "What the hell have you got on your forehead?"

Emmett turned to the judge. "Your honor, I protest. The defendant has lipstick on his forehead."

At Mr. Irving's first mention, Bill used his handkerchief to wipe off the lipstick.

"Stand aside, counselor. Let me see what you're talking about." When Emmett walked to his seat the judge said, "I don't see any lipstick. Mr. Irving, have you been sleeping well?"

Laughter erupted throughout the courtroom, causing the judge to whack the bench he was sitting behind with his gavel. "Mr. Jellico, is the defense ready?"

Jellico stood up and walked briskly to the jury box. "As citizens of this great country you have the privilege of exercising society's right to rid itself of people perpetrating our most serious crime, murder. The seriousness of the crime is only equaled by the seriousness of the punishment. Electrocution in 'Old Spanky.' Twenty thousand volts shooting through a person's body, blowing off fingernails. Smoke coming out of their ears as the brain cooks. It's not a pretty sight, but we only use that punishment on the worst offenders: those who maliciously kill another human being.

"So I'm telling you, if you truly believe that Bill Potter killed his girlfriend and the man he played a game of pool with then, by all means, let's strap him in. But if I can show you how the state's case is not conclusive, that the evidence points to another person, that the witnesses aren't creditable, that the gun was planted, then you will do your duty by telling the prosecutors to go back and find the right person to bring before you.

"Bill Potter is innocent and it will soon become apparent to each of you."

CHAPTER 31—THE MONEY

That evening Bill had the bistro prepare the evening meal for his guests. During the day a hotel employee had sat beside his telephone. If any call came, the person was instructed to say that Bill Potter had not yet returned from the trial. No calls were received. They ate in grim silence. Finally, Jellico asked Bill, "How did you get that lipstick on your forehead?"

"Harriet kissed me there for good luck. Why didn't you tell me? I could have wiped it off."

"I didn't tell you because . . . well, because when I first decided to be a lawyer I read about a case where the evidence was stacked to the ceiling against a defendant. On the day the worst of the evidence was to be presented, this famous defense lawyer smoked a cigar—one he had cork-screwed two steel springs inside. As the prosecution presented the most damning evidence the defense attorney puffed furiously on the cigar. The ash grew longer and longer and longer. The jurors were mesmerized by the length of the ash and couldn't take their eyes off, expecting the ash to tumble away at any moment. As the prosecutor worked harder and harder to impress upon the jury the importance of his evidence, the ash grew to an astounding six inches. The defense attorney objected several times, gesticulating each time by waving the hand holding the magical cigar. Of course the judge overruled his objections, but no one in the jury—or among the spectators—was paying the least bit of attention."

"Was he found innocent?"

"I don't know. The essence of the story is what magicians and thieves have known for ages. If a person's attention is directed elsewhere he won't notice the peanut under the shell dropping off the table or that he is now missing his wallet."

Harriet asked, "Jellico, how do you think the trial's going so far?"

"About like I expected. I didn't have any objections to the coroner's report except for his surmise that it was a .38 caliber bullet that killed Hamelin. Tomorrow they'll put on the stand the witnesses they need to establish Bill's motive."

The telephone rang. Bill picked it up before it rang a second time. "Hello, this is Bill Potter." He listened for a moment then said, "I don't know. Let me ask." Bill looked around the table. All of his guests sat on the edges of their chairs in anticipation. "Would anyone like dessert?"

As the evening continued, Bill's party grew restless. Katy had a sack full of money, Pepe had a young lady waiting, Harriet had plans for patching her failed marriage, and Jellico had a notepad of questions he had written down and now needed to determine their order for questioning the prosecution's witnesses. At ten the party broke up and they all went their own ways.

Faye needed a break. She'd always wanted to write a novel. Until now she'd not devoted the effort necessary to dream up a plot, fabricate a setting, establish a time frame, or draw a colorful cast of characters. But now, locked up and with nothing else to do, she'd been writing non-stop. She started Saturday afternoon when her abductor delivered the items he'd purchased from her list.

Without a window or a watch Faye lost track of time. He'd taken her purse, jewelry, and shoes. What she still had was her sanity and a pen on fire. Faye felt reasonably secure. The door to her room was solid wood and heavy. The deadbolt slid into a metal keeper. It would take more than a kick to pry open.

Sunday morning the kidnapper allowed her to empty the chamber pot in the toilet and wash out the pie pan she used for a food dish. On the way back to her room, carrying her clean utensils and refilled water jug, he handed her another sack of groceries. She was sick of vienna sausages and sardines, but except for a few cans of potted meat, that was all he provided.

It was now Tuesday and he had not knocked on her door. The sardine tins were stinking up her room and the water jug was getting low. Faye walked over to the door and opened it.

"Mister, you out there? I need to make a trip to the bathroom." She waited. No response. "Hey, anyone out there?" Faye crept out of her room and down the hall. In a minute she had emptied the chamber pot, replenished the water, and stuck the trash in a grocery sack he had been using for trash. Faye retreated to her room. Breathing a sigh of relief she locked the door and picked up her novel to continue.

Licking the point of her pencil, Faye paused before adding another line. She wondered what role her abductor played in the double murder. She shuddered. How did Bill happen to have his money? It must be a large amount. I'll bet Bill foreclosed on his family's farm. Yes, that's it. Faye started writing a new chapter with a family cast out by a ruthless villain. Bill made a good bad guy.

Let's see, I'll give the young man a baby sister, a pretty mother, and a father who died defending our country. It's all been left up to the boy. He's got to step into his father's shoes and save the farm. Bill gives him six months to rake up a missed annual payment. The boy works two jobs for pitiful wages. He saves everything he makes, eating only cold biscuits and what he can raid from people's gardens. At the end of the six months he goes to Bill's bank. He has—no, he's short by a small amount.

He asks Bill for another month; he'll take on a third job. Bill yawns, says no, he had his chance. The boy begs until Bill gives in. Bill tells the boy there will be no more extensions and he has exactly one month to get the additional funds or else Bill will take the farm. He already has a buyer. Bill asks the boy if the mineral rights are still intact. The boy is dumbfounded. He doesn't know what mineral rights are. Bill snatches a Prince Albert tobacco can from the boys grasping hand and pours out what the boy has earned so far. Bill writes down the amount on a piece of paper with his signature at the bottom and hands the receipt to the boy. Bill stuffs the money into his pocket.

The boy goes home. His sister is sick with the mother tending to her. His mother has started taking in other people's laundry. The boy goes through the small house ducking under drying clothes hung from lines strewn from pillar to post. In the bedroom the mother is sitting, holding the little girl. The child's complexion is pale, her eyes sunken, her hair matted from laying on a pillow. The mother rocks back and forth on the bed, cradling her baby, and crying. The boy goes outside, he doesn't know what to do. He works late into the night cutting firewood.

Faye stopped writing. "Bill Potter, if any part of this is true, I'll slap you 'till the cows come home."

CHAPTER 32—THE BREAK-IN

"Jellico, the coroner's found a blood stain on one of Bill's shoes. They're bringing back the coroner to testify again."

"I thought he looked at all Bill's shoes and didn't find any blood."

"We asked him to look again—this time with a magnifying glass."

"Whose idea was that?"

"Officer Henderson made the suggestion."

"Damnit, W.W. You know he tampered with that shoe. You need to assign someone else to safeguard the evidence. How can I get Bill cleared if I'm having to work against a crooked police department?"

"Not a department—just one guy."

"You found anything on the disappearance of Faye Spencer?"

"Nothing. She vanished. The pressman was the last to see her. He told her to go home close to midnight and then—puff, she's gone."

"You got any problems testifying?"

"What kind of questions would you be asking?"

"That episode where Raylene slammed the door in the sheriff's face for one. You don't have to say you were a paying customer—just a good friend."

"I'll think about it. This could end my career."

Jellico thanked Chief Wainwright and briskly walked to find Harriet and Pepe. "You two got anything you're working on right now?"

Harriet pulled out her notebook. "We've got a meeting with the switchboard supervisor for the telephone company at ten. Other than that we were planning on listening to you lambaste Emmett's witnesses."

"Good. I want you to have Pepe break into the sheriff's apartment. Don't mess things up. Just find something that implicates him. Look at his shoes, find his bank statements, anything written down, like telephone numbers or names. Leave it like you found it. I don't want anyone to know you were there." By God, if the prosecution wants to play dirty, Jellico thought, I can bend the rules with the best.

"You got it, boss."

Jellico walked toward the courtroom. He stopped and turned. "Why are you going to the telephone exchange?"

"To see if anyone in town has made or received any long distance calls from Chicago."

"Harriet, I don't know much about picking locks. And there are too many people coming and going to give me the required time anyway. I think the best way in is through the window. Most men like to leave a window cracked so air can circulate. With a room on the third floor he probably wouldn't bother keeping it locked, or even closed all the way."

"What about the people driving by on the street?"

"Let's go to the mercantile. I've got an idea."

Two hours later they returned. They parked the Packard in the back and, with Harriet as a look-out, Pepe changed into a pair of overalls and a yellow plaid shirt. Harriet helped him untie a big ladder from the roof of the car and carry it and a bucket of water to the front of the building. Pepe had towels and a squeegee. To anyone walking by, he was a window washer.

Harriet held the base as Pepe climbed the extended ladder. The higher he got the more unstable the ladder became. Harriet was sure Pepe would soon tumble down. They had positioned the ladder between the first window and a drain pipe. When Pepe reached a narrow ledge he grabbed the drain pipe and pulled himself up onto the ledge. With his hands flat against the building, he sidestepped a couple of feet to the first window belonging to the sheriff. It was locked. Pepe shook his head in disgust and continued to the next window. It was open, letting in a sliver of air.

In just a few moments Pepe was inside. He walked to the entry door and unlocked the deadbolt. Back at the window he motioned for Harriet to come up the stairs. When Harriet arrived, they started scouring the apartment. Sheriff Shodtoe would be working all day at the courthouse. They could take their time and do a thorough job. Trouble

154

was, they didn't find anything. One envelope containing five hundred dollars and a telescope on a tripod pointed at Faye Spencer's bedroom window. There weren't any books, no pads of paper, no telephone numbers, no incriminating evidence of any kind. Pepe suggested Sheriff Shodtoe must keep everything worth hiding in his office or squad car. He went to the refrigerator. Nothing much there or in the pantry. Plenty of beer but not much else. Harriet was in the bedroom rummaging through the night stand. A few travel post cards. One comic book about the war, autographed by 'The Calhoun.'

"Eureka, I've found it."

Harriet ran into the bathroom. Underneath a hanging bathrobe sat a lonely house slipper. Pepe had the other held to the light above the lavatory. "There's blood. See that stain right there." Pepe was pointing to a dark stain covering a portion of the deerskin sole. "And it's on the right shoe. Do you think we should take it with us?"

"No. Let's leave everything as we found it and report back to Jellico."

"You want to go down the ladder this time?"

"No, I'm wearing a dress and you just want an eyeful while you hold the ladder steady."

"I thought it was a good idea."

CHAPTER 33—THE PROSECUTION

"The state calls Jennifer Gibbs to the stand."

The sheriff was standing by the entrance door. He stepped outside and in a moment ushered her in. After Jennifer was sworn in and seated, Emmett casually walked over and conspiratorially leaned against the railing separating the two. "Miss Gibbs, will you tell the court what you know about the relationship between Mr. Potter and Miss Carlisle."

"One day Mr. Potter walked to my desk and said for me to start paying Miss Carlisle's rent and utilities every month from his personal account. He gave me the addresses and the amounts to pay. Eventually I had the utility bills sent directly to the bank."

"Miss Gibbs, was there any indication of what Mr. Potter might receive in return?"

Jellico was out of his seat. "I object, your honor. Calls for speculation."

"Sustained. Rephrase your question, Mr. Irving."

"Miss Gibbs, did Mr. Potter give you any details about their relationship?"

"He gave me her telephone number. If there was an emergency and I needed to talk to him he said to call her number. But I was strictly forbidden to call her number on any evening other than Friday."

"Was that because he had a regular sleepover on Friday nights with Miss Carlisle?"

"Objection, your honor. He's leading the witness."

"Sustained. You can't testify for the witness, Mr. Irving."

"Miss Gibbs, what times on Fridays were you allowed to call Mr. Potter at Raylene's apartment?"

"From six in the evening until ten Saturday morning."

"So it was a sleepover."

"Objection."

"Sustained. Move along, Mr. Irving"

"Miss Gibbs, did you ever miss making any of those payments?"

"Yes. I once took the flu and was out of the office during the time I normally paid her bills. I really never thought any more about it until one day she charged into my office and demanded I pay her electricity that very moment. She said, and these are her very words, 'I wonder what Bill would say to you if I cut him off like you cut off my electricity.'"

"I see. And did that mean anything to you—her cutting him off I mean?"

"Objection, your honor. Calls for speculation."

"Overruled. Miss Gibbs, stick to the facts you know."

A general snicker echoed throughout the courtroom. Everyone knew what Raylene meant.

"I don't know, but I do know she was plenty mad."

"Couldn't she have paid it and had you reimburse her later?"

"No. During those first few years she never had much money. Mr. Potter told me to honor all her checks. I was to use his personal account for the cover and for the bank's NSF charges. She must've had a dozen checks written that first year, for more than her account balance."

"I see. Was there anyone else who would step up and bail her out if Mr. Potter decided he didn't want to pay her rent and utilities anymore?"

"Not that I'm aware of."

"Miss Gibbs, did Miss Carlisle ever threaten Mr. Potter?"

"That day, when she came to my office. She sat down while I called the electric company to have her power restored. I heard her mumble, 'I could really fix his wagon.' She then looked up at me and said I'd better get her power back on pronto."

"Miss Gibbs, you are no longer working for Mr. Potter. Would you tell the court why you resigned."

"Bill Potter is a despicable man. I got fed up hiding his nefarious deeds. One time . . ."

Jellico jumped up from his chair. "Your honor. Is this relevant to the case? I'm sure we'd all like to know the mean and dastardly things Bill Potter has done, but if they're not germane to the case at hand they should not be brought up to taint the minds of the jury."

"Sustained. Miss Gibbs are any of these nefarious deeds, these mean and dastardly things Mr. Potter has done connected in any way to the murder of Miss Raylene Carlisle or Mr. Galen Hamelin?"

Emmett Irving stood up. "Your honor, may I approach the bench."

"You may both approach."

"Judge, she's going to tell us how volatile Bill is. She knows him better than any other person. I think you ought to let her testify so the jury will know what Bill is capable of when he thinks someone has wronged him."

"Mr. Jellico, have you any comment?"

"Your honor, Miss Gibbs is not a licensed therapist. She's not an expert in any field. You're asking for her opinion when she can't show how that opinion would be derived from an unbiased collection of previous experiences and study. Letting her continue would be to compromise the trial and give me grounds for a mistrial."

"Mr. Irving, I have to agree with Mr. Jellico."

Back at his table Emmett Irving said, "I have no further questions."

Jellico walked over to stand beside the jury box. "Miss Gibbs, were you friends with Miss Carlisle?"

"Certainly not."

"Why is that? Is it because she is so much younger than you?"

"No. I am a God-fearing woman and I do not associate with the likes of her."

Jellico walked over to the witness box. "Miss Gibbs, how long have you known Mr. Potter?"

"We went to high school together. When we graduated he went away to college and I went to work for his dad. When his father passed away and he came back to take over running the bank, I continued as his secretary."

"During those high school years were you and Mr. Potter in any of the same classes?"

"Yes, there were not many students so we shared most courses together."

"Did Mr. Potter ever take you to any of the school dances?"

"No."

"Did anyone ever take you to any of the school dances?"

Emmett jumped out of his chair. "Your honor. What possible relevance could this line of questioning have to the case at hand?"

"Mr. Jellico?"

"Your honor, bear with me for two more questions and the relevance will be more than apparent."

"Overruled. Two questions, Mr. Jellico."

"Miss Gibbs, have you ever been married?"

"No."

"Have you ever had fantasies of being married to Mr. Potter?"

"Your honor, I object. Miss Gibbs is not on trial here. What possible importance would it make to know Miss Gibb's feelings for Mr. Potter."

Jellico looked at the jury. "Your honor, it is true that Miss Gibbs is not on trial but if she had prejudicial feelings for Mr. Potter and feels slighted in any way because of his relationship with someone she feels superior to then her testimony might be tainted and the jury has the right to know of that possibility."

"Overruled. Answer the question, Miss Gibbs."

There was a hush as everyone waited on her reply. She looked at Mr. Irving for help. She then reached inside her purse for a handkerchief, took off her glasses, and dabbed at her eyes. Jellico looked at the judge.

"I have no further questions of this witness."

The first witness after lunch was Officer Raymond Henderson. After the officer was seated, Emmett strode forth with the suspected murder weapon.

"Officer Henderson, I understand you were the one to find this gun in Mr. Potter's car. Will you please relate to the court the circumstances surrounding its recovery."

"Yes, sir. We had a search warrant to look through Mr. Potter's house and automobile for a pillow, a gun, Miss Carlisle's address book, and a blood-stained right dress shoe."

"That would be you, Officer McRae, and Chief of Police, W.W. Wainwright?"

"Yes, sir. That's correct. Officer McRae went into the bedroom and I went to the garage. The gun was in the glove box, the first place I looked."

"During the course of the search was any other incriminating evidence found?"

"One of the shoes had a blood stain on the topstitching of the sole. Later, the sanitation department found the pillow used to muffle the noise from the gun in his neighbor's trash can."

"Thank you, Officer Henderson, I have no further questions."

Jellico had been waiting for this. Henderson was dead meat. "Officer Raymond Henderson, have you been on the police force a long time?"

"Fifteen years."

"When the city hired Mr. Wainwright for chief of police, did you feel slighted? That the job should have been yours?"

"No, sir. Chief Wainwright is a great chief. He has tons of experience. Me and the others have learned a lot just being around him and watching him work."

"Do you have any brothers, sisters, or other relatives on the force?"

"No."

"How about the sheriff's department?"

"Yeah. Sheriff Shodtoe is my cousin and Rafe and Ralph Johnson, his two deputies, are my nephews."

"I see. Tell me, Officer Ray, the original assessment of Mr. Potter's shoes came back negative. It's my understanding that it was your suggestion that they be looked at again and this time with a magnifying glass. Is that correct?"

"Yeah. I thought they processed them too fast."

"What other duties do you provide?"

"I'm responsible for the documentation and security of the evidence room and all it contains."

"Does that mean if someone wants to look at the evidence they have to get it from you?"

"Yeah, every piece of evidence has a card attached that lists who's checked it out and on what date and when they returned it. I keep those records."

"Does anyone, other than you, have a key to the evidence room?"

"Just the chief."

"Let's talk about the gun for a moment. I see the serial number has been filed off and when I look down the barrel I see tiny filings. Would you tell us any knowledge you might have about this?"

"Sure. Someone used a drill to gouge out the serial number so it couldn't be traced, and they used a wire brush inside the barrel so ballistics wouldn't be able to match it to any slug found."

"Has it been fired after the wire brush was used inside the barrel?"

"No. The scratches inside the barrel are still clean."

"Officer Ray, have you ever heard of a throw-down gun?"

"Yeah. I've heard rumors. When a cop accidentally shoots an unarmed suspect, he'll pull out a gun and throw it down so he can say he acted in self-defense."

"Officer Ray, is this a throw-down gun?"

"No. Absolutely not. I don't know of any officer who actually has one. I've just heard rumors and seen them used in the movies."

"I see. Well, what if I was to tell you this gun," Jellico held the gun high in the air, "this gun is your throw-down gun?"

"I'd say you were loco."

"Well, this gun was used in an armed robbery and in your custody in the evidence room until it mysteriously disappeared."

"Prove it."

"Now really, Officer Ray. Do you think I would make such a statement without proof? Your honor the defense submits the following items into evidence. Item D-ten is an affidavit from Mr. Paul Nelson saying how he purchased the gun from Eberly's Sporting Goods. Item D-eleven is a copy of Mr. Nelson's home burglary report itemizing the gun as one of the items stolen. Item D-twelve lists the gun as entered into evidence in an armed robbery at the Livery Feed and Seed. Item D-thirteen is the evidence ticket listing the people who had possession of the gun until it was returned to the evidence room and disappeared two years later. Item D-fourteen is a sales receipt for the gun from Eberly's Sporting Goods. And last, Item D-fifteen is an affidavit from Herman Eberly positively identifying the gun and explaining how he specially ordered the grips and how he lost one of the screws used to attach the left side grip, replacing the lost screw with a solid brass one from his personal assortment."

Jellico marched around the courtroom holding the gun high in the air. When he reached the jury box, he stopped. "Oh, this is the gun all right. It's your throw-down gun, Officer Ray."

"That's preposterous."

"Let's go back to the time you found it. Did you receive any specific instructions from Chief Wainwright prior to entering Mr. Potter's home?"

Officer Henderson squirmed in his seat. "I . . . I don't remember receiving anything specific."

"Your honor, the defense would like to submit an affidavit from Officer McRae stating that Chief Wainwright told him and Officer Raymond Henderson to work together. Under no circumstances were they to recover evidence on their own. He further states that he was in the lead and went straight to the bedroom, expecting Officer Henderson to follow."

Jellico walked to just a few feet from the witness box. Looking at the jury, Jellico said, "But you went straight to the garage, disobeying a direct order given to you not ten minutes earlier. Explain your actions to the court, Officer Ray."

"I . . . I wasn't paying attention. I wanted to be the first to find something incriminating."

"I see. And you didn't plant that pillow in the trash can across the street?"

"No."

"And when the lab said that there were no blood stains on any of Mr. Potter's shoes you did not use your key to take one of Mr. Potter's shoes from the evidence storage room and doctor it with blood and then ask for the lab to re-examine the shoes?"

"I did not. Listen, this Bill Potter is a real work of art. Let me tell you what he did to a bunch of boys in Wind Springs just a few months ago."

"Your honor. Instruct the witness to answer only the questions asked."

"The witness will refrain from offering opinions or information not requested."

"I have no further questions."

"Thank you, Officer Henderson. You may step down." The judge looked at his watch and announced, "Court is adjourned until eight a.m. tomorrow morning." He slammed down his gavel and left through a side door whispering something to the bailiff.

In a few minutes the bailiff ushered in the prosecuting attorney, Emmett Irving. The judge sat behind his desk with a glass of scotch. "Care for a drink, Emmett?"

"Thank you, your honor."

"Boy, your case is coming apart. I'm thinking of throwing the gun out. What else you got?"

"Henderson is a bungling oaf. Wainwright should have kept him under closer inspection."

"If I throw out the gun I don't think you've got enough evidence to convict. So I'll let it stay for the time being. Have the bank examiners come up with anything?"

"No. He was smart enough to keep his personal business completely separate from the bank's. If you'll let the gun stay I'll have the boys search every inch of that block for the slug."

"No. Damnit, Emmett, were you not listening? The gun's barrel has been razzed on the inside. You'll not be able to prove any slug you find came from it. You need something more along the lines of a witness. Get with it man."

The judge walked over to his door and opened it for Emmett. The meeting was over.

The next day Emmett Irving brought in the witness who saw Bill leave the scene two hours before the coroner said was the earliest the murder could have been committed. He then called Chief Wainwright.

"Chief, did Mr. Potter give you an alibi for his whereabouts at the time the murder was committed?"

"No. He said he came home a little drunk and slept soundly till the next morning. No one lives with him so . . . no, he didn't have an alibi."

"Did he tell you why he was at Miss Carlisle's house on the night of the murder?"

"Yes, he said he was her regular customer on Friday nights."

"Would you elaborate about this customer business?"

"Miss Carlisle was a prostitute. She had a select clientele and charged each one a substantial amount. Each client was allocated one weekday. For a hundred dollars per month Miss Raylene Carlisle made him feel like he was king on his day."

"Chief, how do you know this?"

"I was her Wednesday."

A hush stilled the courtroom. People sat on the front edge of their seat so they wouldn't miss a word. Chief Wainwright continued, "Bill Potter was her Friday. He told me he went to tell her he was discontinuing their long-term relationship. He said she was upset but regained her composure by the time he left, fifteen minutes later."

"Did Bill know she had other clients?"

"Yeah, we all knew. But not their names. She referred to us by pet names. I was 'Pookie,' Bill was 'Sweet Cheeks.'"

People started laughing from all corners of the courtroom. Just think, their upstanding chief of police was "Pookie" and their infamous banker was "Sweet Cheeks." The judge slammed down his gavel several times before order could be restored.

"I know of two others, but not their real names. One is 'Sugar Bear' and the other is 'Daddy Longlegs.'"

"And you have no idea who these two might be?"

"No."

"Did Bill mention why he was breaking up with Miss Carlisle?"

"He said he'd found someone else."

"Do you think Miss Carlisle would have retaliated in some way?"

"No."

Emmett frowned. He stared at the chief, who continued with, "She once told me she lived by three principles. Men are shallow, love is make-believe, and nothing is permanent. To her it was just business. To the four men she shared her bed with she was the most important person in our lives and we only got to be with her one day each week."

Shaking his head, Emmett walked to the prosecution table, "Your witness, counselor."

Jellico walked to the center of the courtroom—equidistant from the defense table, the judge, and the jury box. "Could Sheriff Shodtoe be one of the other two clients?"

"Absolutely not. I got a call from her two months ago on a Thursday night. Shodtoe had been to her apartment . . ."

The chief looked out across the courtroom. Everyone turned in their chairs to look at Sheriff Shodtoe standing beside the entrance door. Shodtoe perspired and shifted his weight from one foot to the other.

"She said he told her he knew what she was selling and if he wasn't given equal billing, he and his boys would make trouble for her. She called him a name and slammed the door in his face. I was given that Thursday for free. As far as I know, Shodtoe never followed through with his threat."

"Let's talk about the gun. Are you absolutely positive you told Officer McRae and Officer Henderson to work together?"

"Yes. That's standard protocol. To keep down any chance of being accused of planting evidence, the officers have to work together."

"Thank you, Chief. That will be all."

As the chief was leaving the witness box the courthouse door burst open, and a filthy woman, tall at six feet or more, and with flaming red hair sticking out in all directions stomped in.

At the top of her voice she screamed, "Where have you all been? I was abducted at gun-point and held for ransom three blocks from here. Someone should have come looking for me. What the hell are my taxes for?"

The wild woman walked barefoot straight down the center of the courthouse, stopping when she confronted Chief Wainwright. "I expected more out of you, Wainwright. You and your Keystone Cops floundering around dressed up like little Hitlers. You think more of your gun belts and every contraption you can get attached than actually protecting someone."

She marched to the defense table. "Bill, was I not worth the price of one small farm? I thought you loved me. You love that damned money. What would it have cost you? Five thousand . . . ten? That's nothing to you. I must mean nothing to you as well."

She turned to the judge and screamed, "Get me something to eat."

The judge brought down his gavel. "Court is adjourned. Bailiff, escort this woman to the Ritz Bistro. The county will pick up the tab for whatever she wants. Bailiff, get a move on; I think she means business."

CHAPTER 34—THE DEFENSE

"Your honor, Sheriff Shodtoe is definitely involved in this case. I'd like to look in his apartment." Chief W.W. Wainwright held his hat in his hands, wringing the brim with each word.

"Chief, are you going on a fishing expedition?"

"No, your honor. I always thought Bill didn't kill Raylene. None of her lovers would do a damn thing to mess up a good deal. Now, I had my doubts about that creep Hamelin and played by Emmett's rules, but now that Emmett's got egg on his face, I'd like to get us back on track to getting the real killer behind bars."

"What probable cause can you give me?"

"I don't know. Jellico made the request. Said the witnesses he has lined up for today should supply you with what you need. He suggested I write up the warrant and you hold it at the bench. If at some time during his interrogation you feel the justification has been met, you can sign the warrant and give it to me for its execution. If Jellico fails you're to tear it up."

"Damn that Jellico, always making a production. You got it ready for me to sign?"

"Yes, sir." Chief Wainwright handed the judge his carefully prepared warrant and left the judge's chambers.

On Tuesday morning Emmett Irving announced that the state rested. He sat at the prosecution table, embarrassed by his lackluster performance.

In a booming voice Jellico announced, "The defense calls Katy Hamelin." Sheriff Shodtoe ushered Miss Hamelin through the courtroom door. With one hand on the Bible Miss Hamelin swore to tell the truth, the whole truth, and nothing but the truth. "Mrs. Hamelin, would you state your name for the record?"

"Katherine Elizabeth Hamelin."

"Are you the wife of one Galen Hamelin, newly deceased and one of the two individuals Mr. Potter is charged with murdering?"

"Yes, that is correct."

"Mrs. Hamelin, for what reason did you come to Dancing Deer?"

"I was running away from my abusive husband. Faye Spencer is my only living relative and I came here so she could help me hide."

"And you arrived in December, 1944?"

"Yes, sir, around the fifteenth, on the bus with David Calhoun when he returned from the war."

"We all remember that day, Mrs. Hamelin." There was a general murmur as everyone in the courthouse agreed. Except maybe the two reporters from the Little Rock *Gazette*. "And what happened on Monday, February 14, 1945?"

"I was lying low in Faye's apartment. About seven that evening Faye came charging in, saying Galen was in town and had beaten up her boss. I thought he'd come to drag me back and became extremely afraid. Faye called a friend of hers who lived across the street to come over and convince me every thing was going to be all right."

"And the name of this friend of Faye's?"

"Marsden County Sheriff, Sherman Shodtoe."

"What was the sheriff told?"

"Faye told the sheriff that Galen was running from some people in Chicago. Last year he ran to Kansas City to hide, dragging me along. I escaped his clutches at my first opportunity and now he's here. She also told him Galen said he'd take me back or else."

"I see. And did the sheriff make you feel safe?"

"Yes, but he wanted to know who Galen was running from. I told him the Canneli brothers."

"Have you told anyone else your husband was running from the Canneli brothers?"

"No."

"Then, as far as you know, only you, your sister, and the sheriff were aware that the Canneli brothers were looking for your husband.?"

"That's correct. I did mention to the police department that he had ties to the mob in Chicago but did not further elaborate or give any names."

"Your witness, Mr. Irving."

Emmett went through a sheaf of papers from front to back and then again from back to front. He walked to the witness box. "Mrs. Hamelin, are you saying you think the Canneli brothers killed your husband?"

"No. They wanted him dead all right, but they didn't find us in Kansas City and I don't think they could have picked up his track to northern Arkansas."

"The state has no further questions for this witness."

As Katy moved to the back door she winked at the sheriff and walked outside.

"The defense calls Beatrice Bentback." A few minutes later Jellico had established that Mrs. Bentback was the switchboard operator at the telephone exchange and that on February 15, 1945, a call was placed from Sheriff Shodtoe's apartment to Chicago. On February 16, 1945 a call was received at his apartment from Chicago. She said an additional call was placed from Shodtoe's apartment to Chicago the day the funerals were conducted on the 22th. It was with this revelation that the judge gave a slip of paper to the bailiff to hand to Chief Wainwright. Emmett had no questions for Mrs. Bentback.

The next person called was Charles Jimmerson, the acting CEO of the First Bank and Trust of Dancing Deer. He testified that Sheriff Shodtoe received a bank wire for five thousand dollars from a bank in Chicago on the 26th of February, four days after Galen Hamelin's funeral. He further stated the bank wire did not list a payor.

With this bit of information, everyone in the courtroom turned to see Sheriff Shodtoe's reaction. He wasn't there. Instead, Deputy Sheriff Rafe, or maybe Ralph, Johnson was minding the door. He shrugged his shoulders when prodded by Officer Steve Trent where the sheriff had gone.

District Attorney Emmett Irving stood at the prosecution table. He said, "Your honor, may I approach the bench?"

"Approach, Counselor."

Emmett Irving and Jellico stood before the judge. "Your honor, the state has decided to *nolle prosequi*. We have not been able to establish enough creditable evidence to continue."

"I agree, Mr. Irving. Do you have any comment, Mr. Jellico?"

"Your honor, I believe Chief Wainwright is searching Sheriff Shodtoe's apartment. He will find a house slipper with a stain that will test as Galen Hamelin's blood. I have no problem discontinuing the trial if that bit of evidence can be included. It's my understanding that *nolle prosequi* does not provide Bill Potter the same legal position as a verdict of not guilty. He can still be tried for these murders at a later date if the state so decides. The standard of double jeopardy doesn't apply. Is this assessment correct, your honor?"

"Yes, I believe you are correct. So do you want to continue, Mr. Jellico? Several of these jurors might find Mr. Potter's previous transgressions substantial enough for them to convict him here. It's your call."

"Let me speak with Bill." A few moments later, Jellico returned to the bench saying Bill agreed.

Both attorneys returned to their tables and started packing their briefcases. The Right Honorable Judge Murphy McAdams slammed his gavel to bring order one last time for this trial. He announced that the state had decided not to continue with the prosecution of William Carrington Potter for the murder of Raylene Carlisle and Galen Hamelin. He thanked and dismissed the jury.

Amid the cacophony, he banged his gavel and said, "This trial is adjourned."

CHAPTER 35—THE PARTY

Bill walked down the sidewalk. He harbored a cheery attitude and charity filled his heart. "John, I'm having a party at the Ritz this evening. Come on down, bring your wife." A few more steps. "Mr. Creighton, champagne at the Ritz at five on me."

"It was a travesty. We all knew you'd come out vindicated of all charges."

"Bless you, Mrs. Hardeman. If you have some time this evening, stop in at the Ritz. We've set up tables with plates of food. I understand the punch is devoid of all alcohol. I'm sorry but you'll probably have to wear one of those funny little hats. Ha Ha."

Bill thought all along he'd be found innocent. He'd had all the faith in the world in Jellico. Now it was time to get on with his life, to take a vacation, to salvage his romance with Faye, and to finish his promised civic works. What a lot of accomplishments he still had on his plate.

"James, have you had dinner yet? No? Come to the Ritz in a couple of hours and fill up on Andre's sumptuous feast. We're celebrating justice. Bring your wife. She left you? Got a girlfriend? No? Well, come and meet someone new."

When he walked through the front door of the Ritz Grand Hotel, several employees held out their hands, others clapped, one let out a wild whoop, and still another wept tears of joy. Bill went straight to the elevator and ascended to the penthouse. He wanted to get out of his business suit and into something more in line with the way he felt. At his walk-in bar he located a tumbler and in a few minutes he was holding his favorite drink—a gin martini. He sat down in a leather chair, took off his shoes, and let out all the air in his lungs. He rolled his head from side to side, took in an expansive amount of fresh air, and bellowed at the top of his voice, "Yes."

Bill jumped up and hastily picked up the telephone. Got to call everyone. A grand get-together. Let's see . . . Faye, Katy, Jellico, that funny little Frenchman, Chief Wainwright, Harriet. God, Harriet was something. And Faye . . . busting loose from her kidnapper. That woman's got spunk. Bill changed into a purple silk shirt and cream linen slacks. He combed his hair and descended to the party in progress.

Everyone who was anyone came. Andre had scads of food prepared and placed on linen tablecloths throughout the restaurant. The chairs were folded and stacked out of the way allowing the throng to drink the champagne, eat the *hors d'oeuvres*, and mingle.

Bill stepped on stage and walked to the microphone. A hush descended on the crowd. "I'd like to let everyone know how proud I am to be an American, where if you're innocent of a crime, our justice system will see to it that everything possible to absolve you will work to set you free. However, those guilty must also receive their just reward. I'm just happy to find myself in the former category."

Bill held up his drink. "Let me propose a toast. To the American justice system."

Bill left the stage and walked through the room. It was full of happy people shaking hands and enjoying companionship with their prominent and high-profile banker. Several people asked if Sheriff Shodtoe would be indicted. So much evidence linked him in some way to the crime.

"I don't know. You should ask Chief Wainwright or Emmett Irving." After about an hour of celebrating, Bill had the *maitre d'* escort his special guests to a banquet room where they were seated.

Jellico said, "I was wondering why the waiters told me to eat lightly. I thought you were being stingy."

"You know better than that. I thought we'd get together and celebrate a job well done with steaks not so well done."

"I'll drink to that," said Chief Wainwright.

With everyone seated, Jellico raised a glass of red wine, "Ladies and gentlemen. We have seen what a wonderful thing teamwork is, everyone working together, no one with a personal agenda. Here's to all of you." Jellico drank from his glass. "I think each one can add something to the kettle of common knowledge. We should probably start with Miss Faye Spencer. Please, Faye, tell us how you escaped and what did you do with your abductor."

There was a round of applause. Harriet translated in hushed tones to Pepe.

"It was a gruesome event. He had me scared out of my mind. He told me that if I stayed in this room and only came out with his permission he wouldn't harm me. He gave me a sack of food. I lived over a week on vienna sausages and sardines. No bath, no bed, no watch. The room didn't even have a window. I didn't know what time or what day it was. I was there ten days and thought it was two months or more. At first he checked on me regularly, then nothing. Several times I crept out of my room into a pitch black space trying to find the bathroom. I knew that if he found me out of my room I would be hurt. As soon as I could I crept back and locked the door. It was only when I finished the book and the last of those smelly sardines that I'd had enough. I stormed out of my room intending on unleashing a world of hurt on the man, only to find he wasn't there. I unlocked the deadbolt with a twist and walked into the alleyway and daylight. I was free. His car was still there. He's probably walking the streets right now wondering how I knew he'd left."

"And you were in the Ghent Building all along? I took a prospective customer in there hoping to sell it," said Bill.

"You must not have made it upstairs."

"No. My prospective customer said it was too dark. We were there for only a short time. We heard this loud click and he thought the place had ghosts or rats. He said he wasn't buying it no matter how low I priced it."

Faye continued with, "Those walls are a foot thick. I couldn't hear anything. It was eerie. And there were only two small windows in the whole building. They were up front on the first floor."

Bill added, "I know. The Ghents were paranoid someone would rob them. They had their bank like Fort Knox hoarding the nation's gold." Bill was glad he was able to let Faye know he'd worked hard to get the money for her ransom.

Chief Wainwright said, "Miss Spencer, Bill came to me last Tuesday. Your kidnapper was supposed to call him on Monday and tell him where to make the money drop. But he didn't call so Bill called me.

I put every available man running down every lead we could find. I'm sorry you had to endure the hardship. What did you do all day? It must've been like sensory overload."

"She wrote a book." Katy proudly announced. "It's called *Murder at my Doorstep*. She solved the case on her own."

"Well, I really didn't solve it. I used the scenario to come up with a plausible solution. Of course all of you are in it—with fictitious names."

"Miss Spencer, who killed Raylene and Galen in your book?" Jellico thought he knew who the murderer was but was interested in knowing if others thought along the same lines.

"I have Raylene being killed by the wife of one of her clients. And for Galen Hamelin, I have an assassin from the mob coming into town. Two murders, two murderers, both at the same time."

"So Bill was innocent in your story."

"Yes. Harriet did it."

Pepe choked on his water when Harriet told him what Faye had said. Harriet had to pound on his back before the man could get his breath back.

Jellico chuckled. "I see. Are there other people believed to be the villain or villains? Let me see a show of hands from the people who think Officer Henderson killed either Raylene or Galen."

No one raised a hand.

"Okay, Sheriff Shodtoe?"

Bill and Chief Wainwright raised their hands.

"Jellico, who else is there? We already have an arrest warrant for Shodtoe. Now you're telling me everyone but Bill and I think someone else did it."

Jellico had a big smile on his face. This is just like he thought it would be.

"Harriet, who do you think the murderer is?"

"Evan Bonds."

"And why do you think it was Mr. Bonds?"

"Who the hell is Evan Bonds?" Chief Wainwright was distraught.

176

"Chief, I think he's one of those Bonds boys I had an altercation with in Wind Springs. He must've found me here. If that's the case then this is a frame-up to get back at me for a gentleman's squabble."

"I've already heard about that squabble. Bill, did you know you put one of them in the hospital where he had to have his testicles removed? I think if he found you he would have done something physical to you instead of your Friday girlfriend."

"Gentlemen. Let Harriet tell us why she thinks Evan Bonds is the murderer."

"Right before Christmas, Evan's two older brothers held up a Chinese laundry. One was shot and the other captured by the proprietor. The oldest Bonds boy was named Terrell. He died from the gunshot wound and his captured brother Gleason went to prison at the Tucker Farm. His cellmate was Daniel Poul, Raylene's boyfriend. Daniel was in jail for robbing Mrs. Goldfarb's house while she was being buried. He gave Raylene the money he found and told her to hide it. She deposited it in a savings account in Willie's bank.

"Raylene wrote Daniel to get him to give the money back. His cellmate, Gleason, read Raylene's letters while Daniel was out planting potatoes. Gleason told his brother Evan to go steal it. Evan was just out of the hospital. When he arrived at Raylene's apartment we think Willie was leaving. If that's true, then he probably recognized the Packard and followed Willie home. He then returned to Raylene's apartment. With his thumb over the peephole she opened the door thinking it was Willie. He probably stuck his foot in, not letting her close the door. From there it was a regular robbery. Pepe thinks she tried to break free, maybe kicking him in the groin. He suffocated her with the pillow. He looked everywhere for the money and eventually gave up.

"Pepe thinks he stormed out the door and bumped into Galen Hamelin trying to figure out how to get in. They probably had words, maybe even a physical altercation with Evan going back into Raylene's apartment for the pillow. He used it to muffle the gunshot to Galen's head and ended up planting it in the trash can across the street from Willie's house. He knew Willie would be a suspect since he was the last one to have seen her alive—other than himself, of course."

"You are very clever, Harriet. I applaud your gumshoe ability." Jellico raised his glass high in the air.

"Actually it was Pepe who put it all together. He's the one who found the hidden compartment with her savings deposit books and address book. He's a wonderful . . . uh, gumshoe, as you say . . . the best."

"You may be right. Katy, do you have anything to add?"

"Yes. Mr. Evan Bonds was the man who abducted Faye. His car is registered to his dad, the chief of police in Wind Springs. Also, he was the man who broke into Bill's house and was beaten up by Mary Jimmerson. She's lucky. When he pushed her, she landed next to the fireplace with her hand resting on the poker. I'm sure he thought it was Bill's house, and before he left he'd take care of Bill for him and his two brothers. When that didn't work, he kidnapped Faye."

"Harriet, ask Pepe if we've left anything out."

Harriet was keeping Pepe informed of everything said. When she asked if he had anything to add he nodded.

"He says there were three beer bottles in the top of Raylene's trash can. He thinks Raylene was killed before the apartment was ransacked. She would not have had beer bottles in the trash on Bill's night, and with the weather so cold Bill wouldn't be drinking beer anyway. He also wants everyone to know that it was Evan who ran us off the road, shooting out the Packard's rear tire."

Chief Wainwright looked at Jellico from the corner of his eye. "Did you know all this Jellico?"

"Certainly. These are my detectives. They reported to me everything they found."

"Then why did you paint the picture to make it look like Sheriff Shodtoe did it?"

"I didn't have to prove who actually committed the crime, only give enough evidence to persuade the jury someone else did it.

"We think Shodtoe saw Evan kill Hamelin from his apartment window. He probably ran downstairs in his house slippers, examined the body, and called the police. He'd already called the Canneli brothers to see if they would pay a contract price for killing Hamelin. They called him back and offered five thousand dollars. He said he'd take care of it. They wired the money anonymously to Bill's bank after Shodtoe sent them a copy of Jesse's paper containing Galen's funeral notice. If I'd brought Evan into the picture, I would have watered down the incriminating evidence against Shodtoe.

"Then when we implicated his cousin, Officer Raymond Henderson. I figured to continue. You can now set Emmett straight and go after Evan Bonds."

"I don't think so. Emmett's blaming me for fumbling Bill's case. He's threatened to get me retired. I'm considering it. Even if I stick around, I think I'll let him wallow in another fiasco."

"You might find it interesting that Shodtoe slid a note under my office door. If he's charged he wants me to defend him."

"That's even better. I think while the force is tracking down Shodtoe, I'll find this Bonds kid and hold him until you want to produce him at trial."

Bill raised his glass high. "I am well pleased with how everyone worked to set me free. Let's drink to a heroic performance."

"One more thing." Chief Wainwright sat down his empty glass. "Has anyone figured out who Sugar Bear and Daddy Longlegs are?"

"Pepe and Harriet found out, from their interview at the telephone exchange, that the number to Daddy Longlegs at one time belonged to Emmett. No one yet knows who Sugar Bear is."

"Raymond, don't be speeding. I've heard the police in Wind Springs are the worst in Arkansas."

"Worse than Dancing Deer?"

"You know it."

"When this is over, me and your two deputies are going to put Dancing Deer back at the top of the heap. We can't have this podunk town best us. Right, Johnson."

Rafe, or maybe Ralph, nodded his head. His two uncles were worthless. He and his brother were always having to bail their butts out of trouble. Now he had to find this Bonds character before they messed things up so bad the whole family would be in jail. "Why don't you two let me off at the first pool hall you come to? I'll listen to the gossip and find out where this Bonds boy is. Will you guys be staying at the Piccadilly?"

"Yeah. You got any money?"

"Naw. Give me a twenty."

179

"Boy, we need to find him real bad." Shodtoe relit his cigar.

Ray said, "I heard Emmett's re-convening the grand jury. They probably got a warrant for your arrest by now. Maybe me too. Johnson, if you find him call us at the hotel and we'll haul his ass back to Dancing Deer. If he's still in Dancing Deer, your brother'll have to find him."

CHAPTER 36—POINTS WEST

Pepe knocked on Harriet's door. "Harriet, honey, I've got good news."

She opened the door still dressed in her nightie. "Pepe, it's eight in the morning. Can't you take a day off?"

"Genevieve says she's pregnant."

"That's great . . . I guess. Did she want to get pregnant?"

"She did. And now I'm free to travel America for the next six months. Come with me. We'll go west. See Yellowstone National Park, the Painted Desert, I want to fish for trout in Montana, see the giant sequoias in California, scuba dive in the Sea of Cortez, see the whales."

"Sounds like fun, Pepe. I have to talk with Bill first. I'll let you know this evening. How are you planning on getting around? Unless we steal the Packard we don't have a car."

"I'll buy one. But we'll take a train first."

Harriet thought it would be fun but first she wanted to give Bill one more effort. Today she'd dress in her favorite red dress. He always had a problem with red dresses. Rose was coming to join her enterprise and bring Carson. If Bill ever loved her, he could again. With Rose they'd be one happy family and back to square one. She couldn't lose. She started the operation with a bath in scented water. She'd made arrangements to have her hair done by the new beauty salon on the first floor. A manicure as well. Leave nothing to chance.

Around one that afternoon Rose knocked on Harriet's door. After hugging, they got on the elevator and went up to Bill's penthouse. "Mom, you look so pretty. Have you and Dad made up?"

"No, honey. He's still mad at me. I haven't been able to break through the ice. He thinks I'm only here to make his life miserable. We'll see how today goes."

"Okay. Today's the day."

When they stepped from the elevator, Rose ran to her father. She hugged him, kissed his cheek, and whispered in his ear. "Tell her you think she's pretty."

"Hello, Harriet. I wasn't expecting you. My, but you do look lovely. I'm sorry I haven't properly thanked you for the work you did for Jellico. I might be in difficult circumstances if you had not stepped in and taken charge."

"It wasn't me. Pepe's the one who figured everything out."

"Maybe that's so, but he would not have been involved if it hadn't been for you. You chauffeured him around, translated what other people said, gave him the clues he needed. No, I owe you a lot."

Harriet's face grew red. She looked down at her shoes.

Bill continued with, "I thought I'd show Rose and Carson the new park. It's almost ready to be donated to the city. It's such a pretty day. Right now they're planting flowers everywhere."

As they left the lobby, Bill made a gesture to the concierge to let him know an adjustment needed to be made to the arrangements. In return the concierge counted three adults and one child and winked at Bill, letting him know everything in the park was ready for four.

"Willie, I'm so glad the anonymous donor had the sidewalks widened. We can walk three abreast, arm in arm, and still people have room to pass. Dancing Deer is such a beautiful town. I don't know why I couldn't recognize it when I was here years ago."

Carson had a wooden airplane. He walked in front, running its motor with his mouth. "Rrrr urrr." He made the plane soar, dive, circle, and land. It had small rubber tires that turned on the cement. He then made it sail down the sidewalk, gradually taking off. In a few minutes he had it flying upside down. The pilot fell out of the cockpit, but the plane kept flying. Harriet retrieved the lost pilot and planned on holding it until Carson realized it was missing.

"I've noticed people using the trash receptacles instead of throwing their refuse on the ground. There's a pride swelling in the hearts of the Dancing Deer inhabitants." Harriet handed Carson the fallen pilot.

"Yes, and all it took was some visionary to see where a little dab of money could be wisely spent."

"Dad, Mr. Calhoun says you know who that visionary is."

"Yes, I think I do, but I can't tell anyone. I made a promise and I aim to keep it."

They walked past Creighton's Jewelers and continued. People along the way spoke of the beautiful day, shook hands, tipped their hats, and tousled Carson's blond locks. When they reached Ridley's Park, they found nursery workers kneeling on green mats planting flowers. One man wore rubber waders. He stood in a small rock-enclosed pond arranging water lilies. He got out when they arrived and went to work in another area of the park.

At one end of the pond in a separate pool was a waterfall. Inside the pool was a submerged pump that pumped water into another pond a short distance away and at a higher elevation. The overflow of the higher pond criss-crossed the park in a narrow rock-filled stream and eventually cascaded over the waterfall back into the pool with the pump. The second pond containing the water lilies received a fresh supply of water when small amounts slid over the rock barrier separating it from the pool with the pump. Beside the lower pond with the water lilies was a wrought iron table covered by a starched white tablecloth. It was set for four, one plate substantially smaller than the others and a rather tall chair pulled up to it.

"Willie, this is wonderful. So romantic. I think I'm falling in love all over again."

The table held silver lids covering bowls of steaming vegetables. Each plate held an entrée. Covered pitchers sat close by on a second table. Rose placed Carson in the tall chair. Bill turned over the glasses and poured drinks. Harriet sat opposite Carson with Rose on her left.

Bill stammered. "If it's all right with both of you, I think I'll wait a few minutes before I eat I want to listen to the water."

Rose said, "Dad, please be seated. I don't know when I've been happier. Well, maybe once. The day David came home."

Bill reluctantly sat down. He peeked under the silver dome over his plate. A ribeye steak, just as he'd ordered.

"Willie, darling, will the donor put lights along the sidewalks and spotlights in the water so lovers can meet at night and plan grand adventurers, maybe a proposal?"

After a few minutes, Bill breathed a sigh of relief and started to eat his meal.

"Willie, what are your plans? Now that the trial is behind you, have you got anything needing to be done?"

"Just those divorce papers."

"Why don't you hold off on those. There might be some development to make you change your mind."

"I don't know what that would be," muttered Bill. A woman walked up from behind.

"I'm so sorry I'm late. I was up till three this morning re-working the ending to my story, and overslept. I've been running late all day."

Bill stood up. "Here, Faye. I was in your seat. I'm sorry, I've even eaten part of your steak."

Faye sat down. "Harriet, Bill didn't tell me you were going to be here. I thought it was just going to be the two of us. And then he called and said Rose and Carson would be here as well."

"I see. I tagged along without asking if I was invited. Actually, all I wanted to say was that tomorrow Pepe and I are heading west. We're going to Wyoming, Montana, Washington State, California—all points west. He wants to see Yellowstone National Park, pan for gold, climb some big trees, and scuba dive with whales. If it's all right with everyone I think I should go back and start packing. Pepe says we're going by train first. Buy a car later." Harriet dabbed at her nose with the napkin and got up.

Rose excused herself and asked Bill if he would look after Carson. She wanted to walk her mother back to the hotel.

"So, Bill. What was the important thing you wanted to talk about?"

"Faye, I thought you and I could start seeing each other. You know, a relationship. I've stepped away from all my skullduggery. I haven't shanghaied anyone in the last several weeks. It's been almost a month since I was involved in anything clandestine. No mayhem, no arson, no armed robbery, no treason. Hell, I'm a clean man. Worthy of a second look."

"Bill, I can't think about that right now. Chief Wainwright and I are headed to New York City. He says he knows some publishers who might be interested in my book. We're leaving in just a few minutes. Do you think you could look after my sister? She doesn't know too many people. Until a month ago she was hidden in my apartment."

"Sure, but what about us?"

"I'll be back soon. We'll see what happens. Toodle-do."

Bill sat in his chair. Sometimes having all the money in the world is not enough.

"Here, buddy. Let Papaw help you with that." Bill picked up the wooden airplane and wiped mashed potatoes and gravy from the tail section. "Carson, tell your Papaw how you think he ought to handle things. He's made a mess on his own."

Carson was down from his seat. He'd seen a bullfrog in the pond and was going to catch it. His mother would be so proud. He'd surprise her. Make her close her eyes and hold out her hand. Before Bill could intervene Carson was in the pond. It was only three feet deep, but in April the water was plenty cold. Carson lunged after the bullfrog and fell headfirst among the water lilies. He opened his eyes and looked point-blank at an amused large goldfish. Bill removed his jacket and waded into the pool to retrieve his mischievous grandson.

"You're going to get us both in trouble." Out of the water Carson started shivering. Two men walked up and started gathering the dishes.

"Did you bring the catering truck?"

"Yes, sir. Would you like a lift?"

"No. I'm taking it. Someone will bring it back in a few minutes."

Back at the hotel, Bill delivered Carson to Harriet's room. "Listen, Rose, I'm sorry about the meal. I planned it yesterday after the trial ended. Your mother wasn't supposed to be there."

"I don't think you'll have to worry about Mom anymore. She's already packed and with that Frenchman. In fact, he told her not to pack, he'd buy her anything she wanted. I think he's wealthy. David says he owns a vineyard in France and exports wine all over the world. He could probably buy you for what you think you're worth and sell you at last week's market price without flinching. Mom said she's got to have a new wardrobe if she's going west. All her clothes are for the east and everyone knows the people out west wear different styles."

Bill moaned and headed to his suite. He changed clothes and drove to Snockered.

"Hello Mr. Potter. What can I get for you?"

"Vodka, neat—double—from your freezer."

"Mr. Potter, the last time you ordered one of those you created a mountain of trouble for yourself."

"Bear, I've got woman problems."

"Don't we all."

The End

Author Bio

Ron Lambert, an examined life

As an accountant in a small West Texas town, I spend my days studying the bank statements and tax returns of other people's businesses. I classify, summarize, and display their financial transactions in some meaningful format. I love creating order out of chaos.

I'm middle-aged and twice married—with the second blessed from heaven. Four grown children, their children, two bobbing tails of barking energy, and one sly cat round out my cache of treasure.

Over the years I have owned and operated two boutique retail stores, several service businesses, one ranch, and one restaurant. I have been prosperous and poor, with wild fluctuations in between. At present, being neither rich nor poor, I consider my status as deeply entrenched in middle class—a term bandied about by politicians and economists.

A few years ago, in an effort to restore my youth, I purchased an old sofa on two wheels. Since that initial existential groping, I have occasionally strapped sacks of clothes, maps, and a compass that doesn't seem to work onto the back cushion. After kissing my wife, I set out for adventure and story and to find answers to the big questions. Usually, after only a week or so, I realize what I left behind was more important than what I set out to find and drive a day and a night hell-bent-for-leather back home.

I then settle into an old and comfortable routine. I read a few books, attend a few plays, daydream of new horizons, and plan my next adventure. I kept a journal on my first excursion. It was such an exhilarating experience: rewriting the journal and incorporating the pictures I took that I became intoxicated to the point I wrote a novel.

At present, with pen on fire, I am writing my eighth book. I'll win prestigious awards and be asked to speak at the local library if someone would read what I have written.

If you're looking for an evening spent with colorful and mesmerizing characters, if you want to immerse yourself in a rollicking good story, enthrall yourself to the point of madness, go two days without bathing, then have I got a story for you.

Additional Novels

The Dancing Deer Story

Soon all will be available in multiple formats at Amazon.com. Trade Paperbacks in perfect binding can be purchased at our corporate office and from display stands in several of our fine businesses in Columbus, Texas

Dancing Deer (Book 1)

Dancing Deer is the embodiment of small-town America. When asked, she sent her sons to war. This is the story of The Calhoun—one of those boys. It's also about his fellow combatants, the men he served, the men he fought, and the women he loved.

There is the French Resistance, the German Gestapo, *Midge at the Mike*, Anzio Annie, the *Gustav Line*, and the US Army's Forty-Fifth Infantry campaigning from Sicily through Italy, France, and Germany to push back the formidable Germans. But this story is so much more.

Find a comfortable chair and settle in with a great new book. You won't be disappointed.

The Last Dance (Book 2)

Bill Potter is charged with murdering his Friday night squeeze. His bumbling lawyer steps out of a dead-end job of contracts and leases to save Bill from being strapped to "Old Spanky." Bill's wife returns after a twenty year absence to muddy the waters and it's up to her and Pepe, the womanizing Resistance fighter and WWI spy from France, to solve the case.

The Measure of a Man (Book 3)

A group of Cuban immigrants decide to barnstorm the Midwest, entertaining the towns they come to with a game of ball. When they get to Dancing Deer the men on the city council con Bill Potter into a wager for more than they can afford to lose. Bill's position is that the Men from Dancing Deer will prevail. With a team of misfits and one win under their belts, Bill goes searching for a new manager. His ex-wife is traveling throughout the Western US with Pepe, the French womanizer. She knows more about ball than anyone and he has to convince her to come back and once again save him from the wolves at the door.

Lost in Appalachia (Book 4)

Dancing Deer's Chief of Police is lost in the mountains of West Virginia. Suffering from an injury, he can't remember who he is or why he's lost. Two kids take him in and hide him from a determined fiancée. The chief of police is in the process of teaching the kids how to read when the fiancée posts a big reward for knowledge of his whereabouts. The chief thinks he must have committed a major crime for someone to pony up such a large bounty. With the children hiding him, the chief has to decide what to do when he learns the shady secrets of an earlier life.

Christmas in Dancing Deer (Book 5)

St. Bartholomew's is consolidating its orphanage, but the children don't want to be separated. They come up with an alternative plan to present to the church, but the women of Dancing Deer bring the orphan girls into their homes for the holidays. The orphan boys leave on their own in the snow three days before Christmas and spend a night with a burdened bank robber in a desolated cabin. This is a classic tale of how good triumphs over evil in an adult sitting.

Beggarman, Thief (Book 6)

A story of a bank robber who finds his moment of epiphany in a shack with six lost little boys. He goes home after twenty years on the lamb to have Christmas with his family and to right his wrongs. But he finds his past is in hot pursuit and the new life he has found is in jeopardy. He runs away in the clutches of a pretty lady evangelist who is taking her show on the road to the very town where he committed his last crime. A story that can be enjoyed by everyone.

Toe to Toe with A Drunken Philosopher

This is really one story in three parts. First we have the high school philosophy teacher who has to resign his position much as Aristotle had to when the authorities in Athens came looking for him.

Part number two is of an indigent Irish family who emigrate from the Emerald Isle. The little Irish boy in the family grows up to become a priest. Then the third part pits the philosopher and the priest in a contest of wits.

Racing the Wind   (Book 7 in the series, but not yet finished)

The story of a boy with plans to someday build bridges or design skyscrapers. He decides to start with a racer in the All American Soapbox Derby. Problems, orchestrated by his main adversary, creep into the racer's production. The boy has to rely on the help of a fellow classmate—a girl—to find the source of his problems and to finish the racer and the race.

Order Form

Book Name	Qty	Price	Extension
Dancing Deer	☐	$17.95	_____
The Last Dance	☐	$15.95	_____
The Measure of a Man	☐	$15.95	_____
Lost in Appalachia	☐	$15.95	_____
Christmas in Dancing Deer	☐	$15.95	_____
Beggarman, Thief	☐	$15.95	_____
Toe to Toe with a Drunken Philosopher	☐	$15.95	_____
Racing the Wind	☐	$15.95	_____

Sub-Total   _____

Sales Tax (for Texas purchases) @8.25%   _____

Shipping: $4.00 for 1st Book
       $2.00 for each Additional   _____

Grand Total   _____

Would you like your book(s) autographed?   Yes ☐   No ☐

Would you like your book(s) wrapped?   Yes ☐   No ☐

To_____ From_____

Order Form (continued)

Name _____

Shipping Address:

    Military APO   _____

    Street or PO Box   _____

    State and Zip   _____

Telephone _____

Payment:

    Check Enclosed   ☐

    Credit Card:

        Discover   ☐

        Visa   ☐

        MasterCard   ☐

Card Number   _____

Expiration Date   _____

Code (on back)   _____

Keep Credit Card Information for future purchases   ☐

Order Form (instructions)

Boxes   Place quantity or checkmark (X) where applicable

Mail Completed Form To:
> Printers Guild Publishing House, llc
> 425 Spring Street, Suite 101
> Columbus, Texas 78934-2461

Or Fax Form to:
> (979) 733-0015

Or Call-In Your Order during business hours:
> (979) 732-2962

For Pick-Up:

You are welcome to come by our office in the Stafford Opera House at 425 Spring Street, Suite 101, Columbus, Texas to pick up your order and save shipping costs or to talk with the author.

Please call (979) 732-2962 to make sure someone will be there.

Security

We do not share any of your information with anyone. We do not keep your credit card information unless you check the box allowing us to do so for future purchases.

www.ingramcontent.com/pod-product-compliance
Lightning Source LLC
Chambersburg PA
CBHW030501260626
47157CB00005B/1600